CAPTURED

TRIBES, #4

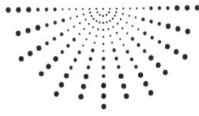

MILANA JACKS

PROLOGUE

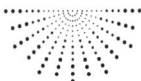

TRIBES SERIES QUICK REFERENCE

*T*ribes series takes place on a planet called Nomra Prime. Thus far, we have the Ka and the Ra tribe that signed a peace treaty after eons of wars. On both sides, females and young are almost nonexistent, and the Ka males are near extinction.

Their alien classification is *Predator*. They're dual-form aliens. Their hunting form is a hunter and often stands as tall as a horse with exposed large sharp teeth, meaning the hunter's lips don't cover the teeth. They have large erect ears, which make them appear bigger and more frightening. They're extremely fit and agile, and can execute leaps we (humans) consider impossible.

Most tribes can be united under a single "King" they designate by adding -i to the tribe name. So for Ka tribe, it's Kai where -i at the end indicates a male who is a leader of the Ka tribe, the top of their food chain and this male always eats first.

Inside a single tribe, an earl governs a smaller territory called an earldom. There can be many many earldoms in any one tribe.

Portal: a spatial shortcut to another place on the planet. A closed portal, meaning a vertical golden line, is not visible to the human eye.

Main Characters:

Hart : Ka tribal leader, Alpha of the Ka tribe. His designation is Kai.

Stephanie: Hart's human. Believed to be Amti.

Nar: Hart's brother and second strongest of the Ka males.

Michelle: Nar's human. Believed to be Aoa.

Mas: Ka tribe portal genius.

Tatyana: Mas' human. Believed to be Eme.

Tis: Mas's brother.

Ark: Ra tribe's Alpha, meaning the strongest of the Ra males but not an elected leader, meaning the Ra do not have a single "King" named Rai where -i at the end indicates his "kingship" over other tribal members. Hart's frenemy.

Sha-male: a male who performs religious rites, sacrifices, prayers (priest, imam, etc)

Gur: Earl in the Ra tribe. Wants war.

Feli: Second to Gur in Gur's earldom.

Nen: Largest and most feared predator. Om tribal leader, Alpha of the Om tribe. His designation is Omi.

The Lore: Tribes worship the female. Goddesses are admired, feared, and respected. They're believed to be returning as human females so that they may walk the lands again.

Bera: Goddess of fertility and war.

Aimea: Goddess of doom. Most feared.

Herea: Goddess of hunt and harmony. Most popular.

Amti: Goddess of madness and lust.

Aoa: Goddess of thunder and pain. Patron goddess of the Ka tribe.

Eme: Goddess of blood and grace. Also called the Bloodletter. Herea's daughter.

Mae: Goddess of fire and lies. Aoa's mother.

Ila: Goddess of wind and desire.

Locations:

Kalia: Ka tribe capital. Near the Ra border. Suffered extensive structural damage during the wars.

Blood Dunes: Ancient grounds haunted by Eme, the Bloodletter. Currently, Ra territory under governance of earl Tash, Ark's brother.

Mount Omila: Om territory. Birds of Prey live here.

TBA as the series rolls ...

CHAPTER ONE

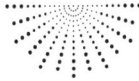

NEN

I spy with my bird's eye something white, round, and unwelcome. It's wobbling back and forth as it floats on the river current that separates Om-ky from the Om-las tribal lands. The Om-las, land predators, are starting to emerge from their huts, creeping down the hill on their bellies.

I whistle to alert my people to the alien object and wait a few moments.

My brother and nest neighbor a short flight distance away doesn't respond, so he's either not home or doing reconnaissance, convinced the Ka are trying to invade our territory again. Turns ago, during the Ka-Ra wars, he spotted one of the Ka pups skulking over our territory, and ever since, my brother has kept an eye on that part of the thick forest, waiting for the Ka to return so he can pick him off.

Where there's one Ka, there're many Ka, and none of them belong on Om lands. We pick off and kill intruders. Maybe ask questions later. Maybe not. This alien pod is intruding. The river current floats the wobbly round thing, and if the current carries it, the waterfall will shatter the pod.

The Om-las seem intrigued and cautious, still descending on their bellies, their red fur making it tough to pick them out in the sea of green grass covered with tall red wild-flowers they've planted for camouflage.

The pod's now floating right under my nest, meaning it's a few thousand notches away, since I live on Mount Omila, the tallest mountain on Nomra Prime. Talons gripping the edge of my landing platform, I fluff up my wings and prepare for flight.

The Om-las are lining up along the riverbank.

The pod's door opens, and I balance with my wings spread as I lean over the edge, turning my head to the side to home in and sharpen my vision. Unfortunately, the door has opened toward the Om-las side, so they can view inside the pod. I observe the land predators' reaction.

On the other side of the river, the Om-las hunters clamp down their large ears and keep their tails tucked under their butts and their legs folded. Their teeth are bared, and they're drooling. They don't appear as if they're gonna attack. They're...tilting their heads as if confused.

I'm dying of curiosity now.

Is there live food in the pod?

A breeze ruffles my feathers, and I fluff them up. I'm not that hungry.

The pod's slowly turning my way, and I'm leaning over as far as I can, shaking my tail in anticipation of seeing what's inside. I spy legs. Chubby, short legs in red shoes with a stick under the heel so the alien walks on props. It pokes his or her head out the door. Brown, chin-length hair, perky nose, and only partly white eyes. Well-fed, I'd say. Would make a nice meal.

It's looking around, probably wondering where it crashed. The Om-las start creeping toward the alien, dipping into the river now, keeping their ears folded, their heads barely above the water as they swim.

Now, most alien species are food for us, and this one looks like a lost food item from space. I haven't had an alien in many turns, and I welcome a change in diet. With a sweep of wings, I take flight, heading for the alien.

The Om-las snap their heads up, their ears perking upright. I assume my targeting position. Wings folded, neck extended, eyes on the food, diving at top speed, wind in my favor. Inwardly, I chuckle. I'm gonna snatch it right out from under their paws.

One of the hunters lifts his head and eyes me with as much malice as he can muster. I bet it's the Alpha of the land Om predators.

Ignoring him, I arrow toward the alien, who's none the wiser. Twenty-three land predators, one sky predator, and this prey is scooping up water and bringing it to its mouth to drink. Tsk, tsk, tsk. Too easy.

One Om-las circles around the pod, practically begging to be seen, but the alien keeps drinking, then retreats back inside the pod. The current picks up speed, surging the pod toward the waterfall. The alien is going to go down with it. Based on what I've seen of the species' anatomy, it won't survive the fall, and since it doesn't have wings, it'll splatter on the rocks. No fun eating that.

The river dividing the land and sky Om is a fair hunting ground. Once the alien makes it to either side of the territory, we respect the boundaries. Eh, most of the time. If I want to eat, I need to move in.

I shriek, alerting the Om-las that I want the prey, and at the same time alerting the prey of the presence of a predator. I hope it'll run, and then I can chase it. The prey pokes its head out and gazes toward the sky. Brown eyes spot me, widen, and it screams at the top of its lungs.

The Om-las use their muzzles to push the pod onto their territory. I drop, as swift as Aoa's lightning. My talons wrap around the pod's opening, and I lift the object, noting it's rather heavy. Straining my wings, I swoop left and away from the river, the Om-las snarling behind me.

I cackle.

Suddenly, the load of the object feels lighter, and the Om-las start snorting, which in hunter means they're laughing. Under me, the alien's running. It jumped ship. Ha! Not boring after all.

I dump the pod and descend, ready to scoop up my food, when the alien ducks. I miss, twisting at the last moment before I crash against the base of the mountain.

Rounding her, I land, inhale a lungful of air, and screech.

The prey, about one-twentieth of my size, fists its tiny hands and screams back at me, then makes a run for a hole in the mountain. If it makes it inside, I'll have to shrink into male to yank it out of there, and that'll annoy me. In male, I'm slow, and who walks when they can fly? Not me.

I snap out my wing and cover the hole, then extend the other wing and crouch. The alien tries to run the other way, but I close my wings around it and bring it to my chest, holding it there while it punches me. I'm eyeing its struggle from above as I sit on the ground, and the Om-las keep snorting with laughter.

Eventually, the prey stops fighting and looks up. Big brown eyes stare at me. They're watery. My food is sad it lost the fight and knows it's gonna die. I contemplate playing with it some more, releasing it, letting it run around just to see how far it thinks it can get. I like playing with food. This one was too easy to hunt, though not boring.

I put the prey down.

It stays in place, even sits, wiping its eyes. It talks at me.

Breasts pressed together to make a vertical line draw my gaze. It is a female prey. With nice, juicy thighs. Mmm.

She keeps talking in a way that requires an agile tongue and strong throat muscles. Her voice keeps rising. Tears flow freely down her face, and she waves her hands about her. Pausing, she stares up at me.

I side-eye her.

She's quiet now, thinking. What's she gonna do? I wonder.

She takes off her propping shoe and throws it at my chest.

It bounces off and flies just past her cheek.

She's trying to kill me with her awkward shoe. I wish I had a translator so I could understand her. I'm sure I'd find it amusing. She doesn't seem to be begging.

Here comes the other shoe, aimed at my head. It hits my beak, bounces off, and falls next to my talon. I flick it and hit the alien in the shoulder.

She throws it back.

I flick it again.

Right at her forehead. Ouch.

She puts the shoe back on her foot and stands to get the other one, then puts that one back on too. The Om-las line their side of the riverbank, curiously tilting their heads. If I leave the prey here, they'll sneak across and consume her. I'm not that hungry, but she looks delicious. A fun and full meal to be sure.

I grab her between my talons, then take flight, her screaming making me happy. I bet she's a squeaker. I love squeakers. Gonna store the food inside my nest for later when I'm real hungry.

CHAPTER TWO

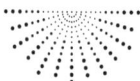

GWEN

T've never been so scared in my entire life. Not when the captain of the spaceship heading to Joylius called an emergency, turning my seat into an escape pod. Not when the pod ejected right before the cruiser exploded. Not even when I thought I'd die crashing on the river. Right now, sitting in the talons of a violent bird, I feel like my heart *will* leap out of my chest.

Too scared to look down and between the talons, I grip them for dear life. The bird's nearing a hole in the mountain. It's a dark, ominous-looking hole. A dragon's lair where it's gonna tear me into pieces. I thought nothing could be worse than the spaceship explosion and crash-landing somewhere, but I was so wrong. This is way worse.

I had no idea these kinds of birds or those hellhound-looking animals down there by the river existed on Joylius. National Security must not know about them, or they would have warned us in case pods had to make an emergency landing far away from where the cruiser carrying humans to Joylius was supposed to land.

The bird lands on one leg, and my teeth rattle from the

impact. I nick my tongue and wince as the bird releases me. Once on the ground, I look up and into its blue under-feathers that soon disappear as the bird moves inside the cave, and not a nest on a tree. This bird is too large to make a home on any tree I've ever seen. It's more like a dragon, living in a cave.

Standing, I take in my surroundings, and my head spins. I pop the pressure in my ears and struggle to get air into my lungs.

"Oh my God." I backpedal away from the sky. Heights scare me. I fly fine because I don't look out the window, but out in the open and at the top of the mountain, I'm terrified. We're so high up, I can barely make out the peaks and valleys rolling beneath it. I barely spot the wide river below us, and I definitely can't locate the pod anymore.

I rub my arms. It's cold up here with the winds picking up and the sun in the descent, and I'm standing in a clearing in front of a cave that's part of what appears to be an extensive mountain range. The landscape below is green, red, blue, and yellow. The evergreen trees appear to have flowers. If Van Gogh painted this, I'd be a tiny dot nobody would notice on the canvas.

I walk the length of the large clearing, realizing pretty quickly I'm trapped. The bird's inside, and I'm not walking into her lair. Although no peeping or screeching comes from the inside of a massive entrance, she could still have hungry young who are sleeping. When they wake up, she'll feed them fresh meat.

Gaze on the horizon where the sun descends, I sit on the cold stone and shiver. Goose bumps rise on my skin. Trying to keep warm, I rub my arms and pull my legs up, then rest my cheek on my knees. Tears cloud the view of a vast clear sky, and I sniff, thinking back to when I boarded the cruiser for Joylius.

Most people went there on vacation, but I practically live in the resort I work at. It's a seasonal job, but it pays better than anything I could find on Earth since bots and robots are starting to replace the majority of service-business employees, and one needs certification to run the bots in restaurants and bars. I've considered moving to a small town in the deep South, where I hear locals still work in the service industry, but the resort on Joylius pays better. I took that job even tho moving so far away from my dad made me feel like I'm abandoning him too.

I sure wish Daddy was here to figure out what to do, because he always knows what to do.

He wouldn't sit here and cry, that's for sure. I wipe my eyes and stand. Turning, I walk smack into the bird's beak, then scream and bolt, completely forgetting I'm thousands of feet above the foot of the mountain.

At the edge of the clearing, I try to stop but can't, and there's a moment of clarity as I fall off the mountain when I know this is my end. My belly rises as I plummet, and I close my eyes. It'll all end soon.

A gust of wind hits my body, and I grunt, the impact stealing my breath. I press my fists to my chest, and, mouth open, I'm a fish, gasping, trying to catch a breath. I hover in midair. I float. Or maybe I died and went to heaven.

The wind gust turns solid (I swear it). It spins me around, pushes at my back, and propels me up. Air enters my lungs, and I inhale, then scream, my back bending from the sudden change of trajectory. My eyes snap open, and I keep screaming as I travel at a speed I can't comprehend. The bird ducks as I fly right over her head and shoot inside the cave to land softly on something.

I inhale and cough. On all fours, I breathe fast, fingers clutching some kind of bedding made of brown fur. I sit back on my heels and press a hand against my heart as if I could keep it inside my chest, unsure if the past few seconds actually happened. I fell from a mountaintop, and I should be dead.

Instead, I'm sitting on a living-room-size bed of fur and straw. It's the bird's nest. Shit. I take a turn about the nest. It's hidden in an alcove between two walls, and light's coming from around the left-hand wall a few feet away.

From the outside, the cave appeared as a dark hole, but inside, tiny lights flutter on walls that are made of smooth black marble-like stone.

One red eye peeks out from behind the corner. The second I spot it, it retreats. I keep watching the corner.

The bird's eye peeks.

Retreats.

She does this several times.

Birds are curious by nature. She's a massive creature, and she's behaving as if she's wondering what I'm doing in her nest. That makes two of us.

She's not attacking me, and there're no young to feed. Her peeking one eye around the corner makes me laugh. Maybe I've gone crazy.

Mom once dropped off a canary we named Boss when Haley and I were small. Mom always abandoned something at Dad's. That's how I ended up at his doorstep. Haley's mom overdosed, and that was even before Dad took Haley in. This bird reminds me of Boss, poking his head out of the little birdhouse in a way that only showed his eye, but kept the beak low.

The bird peers at me again, this time lingering.

On shaky knees, I step out of the nest and whistle at it like I would at the canary. It whistles back, her voice high and scary as fuck. A soprano singer announcing the dramatic escalation of an event in an opera.

I whistle again, approaching slowly, shaking with every

step. Her eye is the size of my fist. She whistles back and sticks out her massive head, extending her neck toward me, sharp beak descending toward my face. Frozen, I swallow.

Her long red beak ends in a sharp tip curved like an eagle's. Her eyes are bloodred, with tiny black pupils. Sharp talons and a massive wingspan suggest she's a bird of prey.

"Here, birdy," I say and whistle again. What else can I do but make nice with the bird? There's nowhere to run.

She mimics my whistle, and I wonder if she's like a parrot, big and scary looking but potentially pleasant, and if I mistook it for a bird of prey.

She exhales in a huff, then rears back and side-eyes me.

I round the corner. The bird sits, puffs out her chest, and spreads her majestic wings. Her wingspan is the length of a basketball court, her feathers blue underneath and obsidian at the top. She's beautiful, if scary, though not as scary now as she was when she hunted me.

Extending my hand, I touch her near her belly, where I can reach. She's so massive that I fit under her when she stands. Her feathers ruffle and tickle my face. I sneeze.

The bird screeches and hops away, closing her wings with a gust of air that almost knocks me down.

"Excuse me," I say. Feeling a sneeze coming again, I pinch my nose, eyes watering. It's coming, tickling my nasal passages. Anticipating it, I bend, and wait and...nothing. Gah, I hate when this happens.

Looking up, I see that the bird's peering at me like I'm a bug.

I sneeze again.

The bird shrieks.

I startle at the noise. She looks mad now. My sneezing annoys her. "I'll try to stop."

Shadows floating over the walls catch my attention, and I walk a few steps around the bird. Behind her is a large pond with steam rising from the surface. The water is a clear teal. Schools of red and yellow fish swim inside this pond, which seems to disappear into the mountain's dark walls farther on the right.

On the other side of the pond is another landing platform that leads to a dark tunnel, and my bet is that's the way out. I search for a way to climb the platform, but find none.

The bird hops onto the platform and settles there, watching me. I walk around the cave, touching the marble wall. It's cold, and the lines that are naturally found on marble on Earth, here appear to be deliberate repeating patterns, not something naturally occurring. Stepping back, I realize they're some sort of writing or drawings, maybe, and the lines are…feminine, even sexy, if that's possible.

In my spare time, I do calligraphy, so I recognize a hand-drawn pattern, perfectly symmetrical, yet if you look closer, you can detect the movement of a hand that's not robotic. That's the beauty of art made by a human and the ugliness of art made by a robot or an algorithmic digital bot. Human art is flawed.

Right before my eyes, a tiny light ignites. I lean in for a closer look. It has tiny wings. Oh shit. I back away. It's some sort of glowy insect, a firefly-like creature with a transparent body that lights up, putting all its internal organs on display.

Wait a second.

I take a long hard look at the "lights." They're all the same, so they're all bugs. Thousands and thousands of bugs on the walls. My skin crawls, and I scratch my arms, feeling like they're crawling all over me. Eww.

"How can you stand living here?" I ask the bird.

It whistles, forming a sound into a question that I interpret as *What?*

Moving away from the wall, I go to sit by the pond and dip my toe in the water. Hissing, I pull it back. "Hot," I say and try again, hissing the entire time my foot makes its way into the water. The bird mimics my hiss, and I chuckle.

She repeats the chuckle.

I laugh.

Feet in the hot springs, I wiggle my toes, watching the fish lazily swimming and the bird's reflection on the surface. I kick my feet, creating ripples while the fish gather around my foot when the bird's reflection shrinks. I stop splashing, and the reflection shivers on the subsiding waves before clearing up. The reflected creature is tall, broad, and stands on two feet. Oh my God!

CHAPTER THREE

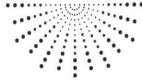

NEN

The prey I was gonna store for later fell from my nest. I contemplated if I would expend the effort to save it or not, and by the time I made the decision not to save it, the wind on this clear warm cloudless day came out of nowhere and swept her tiny body back up.

That is not all the wind did. While I was making the decision whether to save it or not, the wind blew at my back as if pushing me to take flight and rescue it. When I made no effort to retrieve the food, the wind gusted past me and dropped the alien deep inside the cave on the nest. The nest that's never been used, not by me or any Omi before me since…since Omi Mer, the last Omi to have bred Ila, the goddess of wind and desire.

I, like the Omi before me, upgrade the nest once a cycle, but Ila has abandoned us, and the nest upgrading always feels pointless, especially because I don't breed other females and thus have no use for the nest. The Omi is an Alpha male who dedicates his life in service of Ila, the patron goddess of the Om tribe. Since Ila has abandoned the Om, the Omi males have died, never to reproduce or touch a female. It is not possible for us to breed another.

I've existed as a bird for the better part of my life. The bird watches the sky and terrain, flies, eats, sleeps. The bird is simple. The male is not.

The male has painful needs I couldn't sate. Needs like fucking and affection, needs better forgotten if I want to survive without falling off the cliff myself and never spreading my wings.

While Om males seek out females, even our females have been affected by Ila abandoning us. They cannot go into heats. Therefore, they cannot conceive young. During the latest decade-long wars between the Ka and Ra tribes, when Bera reigned not with her fertility gift but with her gift for war, we have all suffered.

The stupid land predators and their wars. Instead of mating their females, empowering Bera to bless them with fertility, they've empowered her to bless them with wars.

The Ka have no females left at all.

We have seven.

The Ra have more, but I hear they're infertile and have grown feral, refusing to even participate in their games.

One would think land predators at war and on the other side of the planet wouldn't affect us at all, but our goddesses connect us by blood, by power, and by food.

I retreat from the alien to clear my head. My body convulses as if something is forcing my transition. Bones move and rearrange. Talons turn into feet, feathers to skin, wings to arms, beak into a nose.

Inhaling, I stare at my hands and claws that are too long to make a fist around my beard, which reaches my navel. My hair's past my ass cheeks. It's been...over two turns since I walked on two feet.

How did this happen to me?

I am a bird, not this slow bipedal male.

Cautiously, I take my first step and wobble, my knee forgetting it has to bend. I take another step and another while the female wiggles her toes in the water. I count the toes. Ten. Huh? Ten toes. What has ten toes, rides the wind, won't let me consume it, and forces my transition from bird to male?

A goddess.

Nooo. That can't be right. Wary of the alien female now, I lean in and count her toes again. Ten. I want to eat one to reduce the number to nine.

I catch my own reflection. I've never seen an uglier Om than myself right now. Overgrown beard, hair sticking every which way, beady red eyes, not the white ones of a male. I'm practically half bird, half male. A feral, ugly bastard.

I want my bird back.

I push my bones out, and nothing moves. I do it again, and fear makes me stop. She's controlling me. Holy...Herea, goddess of the hunt. She's the only goddess with control over hunters. And even though she mainly controls land predators, birds aren't off-limits to her.

Is it really Herea? A shiver runs down my spine. I hope not, and if it is Herea, I'm flying her to the forest near the Blood Dunes where she belongs. Ark, the Ra Alpha, can have her.

The female gasps, and I retreat from the light before she sees me. She'll fall into a coma from the sight of my unkempt self. Can't have that now. Gotta clean up, get a translator, and tell my brothers a goddess who shall remain a mystery walks the lands again. As I search my home for daggers to shave with, Ila comes to mind.

She rides the wind.

And if she desires a male instead of a bird, she'll force my transition. Or is it my desire for the female to be Ila?

Goddesses play with predators the way chicks play with insects.

It's not Ila. That's my hope, and I need to curb it and stop being crazy. But in case it is Ila, I grab a dagger and check the edge. Dull. Gotta sharpen it. Sitting down, I strike the blade in this dark room where an Omi should hold his court. I'm gonna shave, dress up, and present her with my fitness. My chest expands as if wind has entered it, and I hoot, blowing out a cold breath.

The scriptures on the walls of my home say that when Ila used to enter her heat, she would stand on the platform and put out a mating call for the Omi to serve her. The wind would carry the call, and no matter where the Omi was in the lands, he would hear it and come.

I frown. Wait a moment. The alien whistled.

Pausing my sharpening, I stare at the blade. She whistled, and I whistled back. Was she calling me? I better hurry up and groom myself, maybe do my hair with white feathers today. White feathers identify me as the Omi.

Where did I store the white feathers? No clue. My body isn't ready for viewing, but I better make it so, or Ila will suffocate me and get herself another Omi.

CHAPTER FOUR

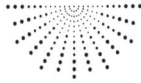

GWEN

*S*cared of the male image reflected in the water, I scoot back until my spine presses against the cold wall while I frantically scan the place. There's only one entry into the nesting area, and it's the platform where the male stood. Nobody stands there now.

I'm seeing things that aren't there. It's just me and the bird. I'm okay. I'm going to be okay. I practice deep breathing.

My heart stops hammering, and when I think all is clear and I've been traumatized enough for one day, I yawn, mind and body crashing all of a sudden. I need a place to lie down. Although the water's hot, the ground is cold, and my ass is almost numb from sitting on it for only few minutes. Better hit the bird's nest and hope she doesn't mind sharing it with me.

I crawl back to the nest of fur and straw and cover myself, leaving only my head above the warm pelts. I admire the art on the walls. Swirling patterns of this kind require an expert artist. Incredible. Hand-drawn, I'm sure of it, though I've never seen anyone stroke the canvas with this kind of skill, and the wall isn't even canvas.

My eyes droop. God, I'm tired, and it's nearing nighttime. It's also freezing. My nose is numb, and I rub it before diving completely under the furs. It smells...warm and cozy, inviting me to stay and sleep. It's not dirty and stinky as I expected it to be.

I drift off to sleep.

* * *

Something soft tickles my cheek. I rub my face, noticing my nose has warmed up from last night. As I scrub my face, my fingertips touch soft fur. I don't remembering it being this soft. I pry open my eyes and rear back. Feathers. Blue feathers. I take a look at my surroundings, down the length of my body. I think the bird's lying on top of me like I'm her egg, and she's keeping me warm. Aww.

I pet the bird. She's sweet. Kept me warm all night. And oh, her feathers are plush and remind me of the fluffy pillows in high-end hotels. Not that the bird would appreciate being killed to fill those pillows... "Thank you for keeping me warm," I say.

She shuffles, lifts a wing, and bends her neck, peering at me with her one red eye. When she blinks, her eyelids close sideways. I blink back at her slowly.

She does the same, equally slowly.

This bird is pretty cool. Not like a pet, though I'm starting to think she thinks of me as her pet or maybe her young, because I'm so small compared to her, and she's keeping me alive. Which is great, if a little odd, but I crash-landed far from Joylius's mainland, and until National Security finds me, I'm gonna stick with the bird.

"You're a pretty bird," I tell her and run my palm over her feathers.

She peeps at me.

I whistle, frowning at the pain in my belly. I think I'm hungry, though the pain is unusually lower than the stomach area.

The bird whistles back.

Sitting up, I smooth out my shirt. "Will hook for coffee," I tell her.

She cranes her head. *Peep?*

"It's an expression saying I'll have sex for a cup of coffee, meaning I really want it. We drink that in the morning over on Earth."

The bird is a great listener, and I'm happy talking at it. Standing, I stretch, and the bird leaves the nest to shake out her wings and tail, then rounds the corner. I follow her to the pond, where she dips in, shaking her butt, splashing water everywhere. She shrieks at me, and I think she wants me to get in with her.

When I don't, she shrieks again.

"Okay, okay! Jeez, take it easy."

I undress and hop in. "Fuck!" I scramble out. "Hot hot hot," I tell the bird. I forgot that yesterday, I dipped my toe and almost boiled my skin. "See? This is why I would hook for coffee. It clears my head, and I can actually function and not dive into near-boiling water and cook myself."

I try again, this time sitting down and going in slowly as one would slide into a hot spa.

Gradually, my body adjusts to the temperature, and I sigh, leaning my head back on the edge. I spread out my arms to hold myself up and close my eyes. "You have a really neat home," I tell her. "People over on the mainland would pay a fortune for a room like this one. Private and secluded. I bet

Mafia kingpins would come here and hide." Either the Mafia or some of the people governing our great nations.

Corruption is running rampant on Earth. It's even worse on Mars, they say, especially in the colony run by Sonfer. He's said to be like Napoleon Bonaparte, obsessed with conquest. And while his obsessions got mankind our first colony on Mars, according to the media—which is partial to Earth since we've been at silent war with Mars ever since they decided to start recruiting their own alien warrior races for their own exclusive use, whatever that might be—he's grown more ambitious.

"I hear the Martians are gonna buy Joylius," I say. "If you could talk, I bet you could tell me all about it. You see a great many things from up here. Oh, hey…" I look up and gasp.

A man stands inside the pond.

He's humanoid, tall, with tanned skin and pitch-black hair and a long nose that tips down. Nude, his abs were made for running my palms over. His facial features are strong, and he's got red eyes with tiny points for pupils. Black eyeliner extends past the corners of his eyes, over his upper eyelids. Above that is a thin blue line.

His makeup is feminine but also sexy, and with blue-and-white feathers and beads interwoven into his long hair, his striking appearance makes me think he belongs in this cave and this region, from what I've seen of it so far. There's a wildness about him.

I don't dare move, but I throw a quick glance at the platform, where I see no bird. Where is my bird now? Why is this man invading her nest? How can she not smell him and want to kill him?

"Greetings, alien," he says, voice deep and rough as if scraping his throat to produce sounds.

"Greetings," I mutter. The pain in my belly shoots straight into my core, down my channel. Swallowing, I sweat and bite my lip so I don't yelp. Oh boy, I'm hurting down there. I'm gonna get my period. Eeeeek. I have no pads. Wha… Oh, come on. That's the last thing I need to deal with right now.

"I am Nen," he says.

"Gwen. I'm Gwen."

He shakes his head. "I don't think so."

"Wait, hold up. Why are you not talking in English?" I ask. Good heavens, I've only just now realized he's not speaking English, and all the Joylius natives wear translators to match our language, not theirs. This means his words translate to English to me so we can communicate.

"English is not our language," he says.

"Should've woken me up when you installed me with a translator. It's a violation to install a translator when the person is sleeping. You're supposed to ask for consent."

He quirks an eyebrow. "You'd have frozen had I not lain with you, female, so *thank you, Nen* is in order."

My eyebrows shoot up. "The bird kept me warm. Where is she?"

The male throws his head back and gives a booming laugh that echoes in the vast cave.

Sweat from both the heat of the water and the pain I'm trying to understand coiling in my belly breaks out on my brow. I wipe it with a wet hand. The male's not threatening me, and he's keeping his distance, so I'm less afraid than I was before.

However, I wish I had a towel I could slip into so I could linger at the side of the pool while chatting with this male alien, who's plenty handsome in an Old Norse way.

On Earth, we don't see guys like him anymore. Beards. Tattoos. Norse biker types like my daddy, though Nen is much younger and, obviously, not my daddy.

I glance at his arms, which dangle from the edge on

which he's leaning his elbows. They're tipped with claws. On Earth, we don't see guys with claws either.

"What's so funny?" I ask when I see he's smirking, red eyes twinkling.

"You think the bird is a female."

"Bird. She. Kind of easier than calling her 'it.'"

"It's a he. Definitely a he."

"Good to know. What kind of bird is it?"

"A bird of prey."

Hm. "I'm fine with it, then? Is it keeping me as a pet or food or both?"

"He likes pets. He won't consume you."

"Is there a name for this family of birds? Like eagle or hawk or some such?"

"An Om."

"Om. Like ominous and menacing. Very cool."

"Like Omega. He is an Alpha male in the true sense of the word as it applies to his mating. Also, you should know he's the largest predator in all the lands."

A bit uncomfortable with the male bringing up mating, I swallow, thinking about the way he used the word predator. A predator species in the context of birds of prey isn't the same as a predator-class alien. On Earth, species classified as predators are dual-form aliens, where one form is an animal that predates on humans. A bird of prey is a bird that predates on other animals. That's all. "Pretty cool. And do your lands have a name?" I'm trying to understand where I landed on Joylius. I wish I had a map.

"Mount Omila and the surrounding territory belong to the Om tribe."

"A tribe. Wow, I've never met a tribal member. Didn't even know there were tribes on Joylius. How very cool."

He doesn't respond, and his gaze becomes unnerving, borderline sexy, making my breasts feel like I'm carrying melons. Good heavens. "So, Nen, what do you do for a living?"

He frowns as if not understanding my question, so I clarify. "A job? Maybe like a farmer or a lumberjack, or maybe you travel to the mainland for work? I work at Majestic." When he doesn't recognize the name, I clarify. "It's a resort." Nen stares at me. I keep going. "It's just that I'm thinking a man who lives out here must be into farming or tree work since that's what I saw when I crashed. Maybe fishing. There's a river down there."

"Fishing," he says and nods. "I fish and watch the territory."

"What do you mean, 'watch the territory'?"

"I keep an eye on the land from up here, making sure no other tribes trespass, making sure the skies are clear of flying objects like your pod."

"Yeah, I hear you. Unfortunately, the cruiser ejected me before it exploded, and I ended up here through no fault of my own. I thought the bird would eat me." I laugh. "She just wanted a pet, a companion. I mean he. Sorry." When he doesn't say anything, I wait. He stares at me.

I stare back, but not at his face. His body is flawless, his muscular definition incredible, and try as I might, I cannot stop perusing his physique. Pain zaps my middle, and I wince, holding the place above my mound. I'm gonna start bleeding in the water. I need to leave. "Do you happen to know a way to the mainland?"

"I do."

"Great. This is great." I smile, excited. "Do you think you could show me the way?"

"Of course."

"Oh man, I'll owe you big-time. I've got some money saved up, and I'll pay for your time."

He quirks a lip. "I don't need currency. We, the Om, are self-sustaining and have no need for trading."

It's my turn to frown. "You mean you don't work for money and buy things? That can't be true. Your jewelry is wonderful. Looks like gold. Is it?"

"Gold..." he repeats, and I can see he's thinking. Sometimes translators take a while to find the correct word or a meaning, so I bet he's looking for the linguistic equivalent to gold on Joylius. If he'd installed one of our translators in himself instead of giving me one of theirs, he'd have no trouble understanding gold. But it is what it is.

"It is gold, yes. We call it something else now. Your dialect is ancient."

Um, no, his translator must be outdated. "How did you get the jewelry?"

"I made it."

"Get out."

His eyebrows shoot up.

"You know how to craft gold pieces and you're not selling them? Some of us humans"—I point to myself—"pay fortunes for hand-crafted items like the ones in your hair. I can envision popular designers paying for this kind of work and selling it for millions."

"You seem overly excited about currency."

"That's because our world revolves around money, and I don't have much of it." I glance at the water, stir it, and collect a wiggling fish in my palm. I drop her back. "I don't know how much you know of our politics over on Earth, but it's not looking good for us. The Martians have robotized everything and are manipulating all the new tech we get from the warrior-class aliens. They're progressing while we regress. Farming, for example, and lumbering are almost extinct. So to eat, I work on Joylius. Here, they pay well and still keep a human labor force. That's gonna change one day, but hopefully not in my lifetime."

"And what have you done in your lifetime?" he asks.

"Not much, to be honest. I wing it day by day. I'm pretty good at calligraphy, but that doesn't pay since people barely write by hand anymore. And like I said, I work at Majestic." I'm feeling terribly unaccomplished right now, and I blush.

"I've also spent a lifetime winging. We have that in common." The male pushes off his end of the pond and moves toward me, flinging his arms up and down, mimicking a bird in flight.

"Stay back." I prop my palms on the edge so I can get out faster if I need to.

His gaze dips to my breasts for the first time. He's kept his eyes locked with mine during the entire conversation. What the hell does he think he's doing now? Why couldn't he stay on his end? I'm nude over here. He's nude over there. And things can go wrong if our bodies collide. Or right, judging by his looks, but I'm trying not to find an alien of another species incredibly handsome. It's taboo. Humanity doesn't mix with other species.

The male slowly treads water, and I stand on alert.

His nostrils flare. "It's best if you don't fear me so much." He's on me in a flash. Palms slam on the stone on either side of my body, and I cover my breasts. He's staring into my eyes, and I his, and his are red, and the paint on the eyelids is not eyeliner. It's just how his skin is colored there. I scan his face as he's scanning mine, as if we're trying to see each other, note the differences up close, and because he's not attacking me yet, I swallow and try to figure out how I'm gonna defend myself if he does attack.

Nothing comes to mind.

"Don't hurt me," I whisper.

He smiles as he runs a claw over my cheek. "You don't want to be hurt. You haven't returned for Bera's war."

I don't understand what he's saying. It's one of those rare moments where I don't know what to say. My pussy, however, is pulsing with a beat of her own. The pain in my belly feels like I'm carrying a ball of molten lava inside. My entire body burns. The baths aren't even hot anymore.

"Which female has ten toes, can't die, can force me into a male, and goes into heat when she wants her Omi's knot?"

"It's not Gwen, I assure you."

"You are Ila, goddess of wind and desire. You've returned to mate with me so that our tribe can prosper." He shudders. "We have prayed for eons, and Ila never came. We lost hope. We forgot our ways, but you are here now, and I will serve you in any way I desire and all the ways you desire as well. I promise I will not disappoint."

I shake my head. "You've mistaken my identity."

"Hmmm, perhaps in your new body, you don't remember."

"Dude, I've had this body since birth, and apart from the first few years of life, I remember everything. Believe me, I'd remember if I were a goddess. It would be hard to forget." I push at his chest, but he won't retreat. I push a bit harder, and he smirks and takes my palm, then runs it over his chest and abdomen and makes me feel the peaks and valleys of his hard muscles. My pussy pulses with need, and I clamp my thighs together. If he wasn't standing in front of me, I'd bend over in pain. A whine slips from between my lips.

"Omega, I can make it better," he purrs. It's a strange sound, almost like a song.

"Where is my bird? What did you do with him?" I want the bird back so he can chase him away. I bet he would. I'm his chick. Birds don't take kindly to people coming around their young.

He settles my palm between his pecs and, with his mouth closed, whistles from his chest in the same tone I whistled at the bird.

"You've been watching me," I say. Stalker!

"Oh, my beautiful, clueless alien female, the goddess has not been kind enough to impart her knowledge, only her spirit."

"I don't understand what you're saying."

"Funny, because you're speaking my language without a translator."

CHAPTER FIVE

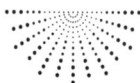

NEN

*T*he female resists both the notion that she's Ila and her Omega dynamic. Her whistle is a mating call. Ila called for the Omi right before she entered the period of fertile time known as an Omega heat. The scent she emits draws me in. But the female also fears me and smells like prey, something I want to eat, which is confusing.

I've never scented such a combination, nor have ever met a creature like this one. Because she is Ila. And despite my shortcomings, Ila has chosen me for breeding, or she wouldn't have displayed her Omega dynamic in such a blatant form.

The moment I opened my mouth, her pussy flushed with the nectar only an Omega can produce. I would smell it even if she was strolling down by the river thousands of notches away, let alone from this close. I am not mistaken. The scent calls to my primal needs, the ones only Ila can sate.

Besides, the knot at the base of my cock is swollen now. It wants to blow up inside her sweet pussy and lock our bodies in a tangle of limbs and fluids. My knot knows. It won't swell for Beta females or any other Omega female besides Ila.

This is her. The alien is her, and this moment in time shall be recorded in the history of my people. After thousands of Omi, Ila chose me. Why me, I don't know and don't care. I care only about sating our desires for breeding.

But before I rut over her, I need to ease her fears. The smell of a prey animal in terror is spreading through the cave like Mae's wildfire. "Curb your fear, Omega." I sniff her hair.

"I will if you release me."

But I don't want to release her. Her body's soft, her breasts plush, and she smells divine, unlike anything else on the lands. The alien I hold is a miracle, and miracles are the goddesses' work, and I dare to hope Bera's reign of war has ended. Maybe even Bera walks again in the body of this beautiful and irresistible female. She is Ila's mother, after all, and will bless Ila with healthy, strong offspring, and many, many heat cycles. Or so I dare hope.

I lift Ila by her hips and seat her on the ledge of the baths. I remain standing in the water. This puts us at eye level, so I'm not towering over her. The subtle change in physical position should ease her terror.

Like all the other prey I've stored at home for later consumption, Ila eyes the exit. Most of the time, I eat out, but this is what prey does when I bring it here. The prey tries to find a way out. There's isn't one. A predator is a creature designed to corner prey. We don't leave exits.

This female is both a goddess and prey. She exists to be fucked and consumed. Confusing me, tempting me, making me crazy with hunger for both her flesh and pussy.

My gaze drifts between her legs. They're slightly open, and because I'm a bird, my vision is keen. I can see the Omega nectar leaking out of her hole.

I want to lick it.

"You are aroused," I say. "But you're covering your breasts, and it's confusing me." I touch my eye. "I can see how your body responds. Fear. Arousal. I also smell your heat and clearly heard your mating call." I whistle. "Your dialect is very old, too old to be spoken by regular folk. You are Ila, and you rode the winds."

"I am speaking in English, and I did not ride the winds. The winds here are so fast and strong that they carried my small body. So no, no goddess here."

"Denial won't change who you are."

"But I can hear myself speaking English!"

Poor alien. I wrap my arms around her. "Shhh. You're becoming hostile. It will rouse the worst in you, I'm afraid. The winds are powerful, and hostile Ila isn't someone I want to keep." If Ila threatens the survival of my people, I'll regret consuming her, but I don't like hostile goddesses. They're powerful and can strike out in anger. I won't be dying anytime soon, not now when I have an opportunity to breed the Omega female, as alien as she might be.

Ila pushes at my chest.

I tighten my hold.

She pushes again, tries wiggling, and I bring her closer still, pressing her soft breasts against my chest. My knot swells more, and I groan into her hair. "I won't hurt you. But I want you to become familiar with my touch, for you will enter your heat, and your need will override your senses. Better to get acquainted with my body now."

A small finger brushes my side. The touch is lighter than a brush of my feathers, prompting my cock to leak semen. I tuck a claw under her chin and lift her face. It's stained with tears. *Do not taste her. Do not.* I stick out my tongue and lick, tasting. Divine. In the water, my cock spurts more semen, and I want to rub it over her ten cute little toes.

Her breathing picks up, so I can hear she's noticed my cock and my fitness. This is good. She's drawn to me, yet confused, much as I am, but for different reasons. I scare her, and my job is to ease her into her new life.

Unlike the land predators, we're not fond of games. Lyu, goddess of games, is not a goddess we admire or pray to. We have our own goddess of sky and of starlight, and we have Ila, an Omega Prime goddess and patron goddess of the Om tribe. It is her I'm hosting. "It is a great honor to host a goddess. It is the greatest honor for an Om to touch Ila."

Her mother, Bera, is the most prayed-to goddess in all the lands. The tribes who wish to breed and conceive young pray to her. This also makes Bera one of the most-powerful goddesses. But Ila is the essence of my people, and we pray for her coming more than we pray to Bera.

"My tribe is Om, from the word Omega. This very mountain, Omila, is named after you. I am sure of your identity even if you aren't. Never fear, you will soon come into knowing of who you are. Ila will care for you, human. I will care for you. You belong here."

"A goddess," she repeats. "I wish that were the case. If I were a goddess, I would have superpowers and could whisk myself right on out of here."

I grind my teeth, fiercely detesting her mentioning leaving. She can leave whenever she pleases. Ila rides the winds. One time, when Herea was giving birth and bleeding uncontrollably, she called for Bera, Ila's mother. At the time, Bera was on Mount Omila and not in Ra territory and needed a way to get there quickly. Ila flew her mother on the winds, freezing the tropical parts of the Ra lands in an instant, causing people to flee the storms.

If she doesn't know her power, I'm not gonna tell her. "If you wish to go places, all you have to do is ask, and I will take you anywhere."

"I wish to eat."

"Of course." I expected something else. Maybe something like *Nen, I wish to breed*.

I step away from the female, and she sighs, no doubt in relief. It annoys me she's relieved. An Omega, goddess or not, ought to beg for my knot to fill her. I smile, thinking of how she'll be begging in her heat. "I will hunt something fresh for you."

"How?"

I frown. "By hunting."

"Right. I get that. How will you get off the mountain?"

By flying is at the tip of my tongue, but for some reason, instinct tells me the female has no idea I'm the bird and hasn't even considered the possibility I am both a bird and a male. Perhaps she's unaware that such a thing exists. I will tell her after I feed her. "I will use a portal." There's one right behind her. I have three inside the home, but have no need of them. Why walk when I can fly?

Her eyes widen. "Like a special opening to another place that's not here?"

"Yes."

"Where's the portal?" she asks, seeming excited. Odd Omega. Very odd. The portals excited her and yet the prospect of riding my knot didn't.

Hopping out of the bath, I approach the nearest portal and point at the thin pale yellow line stretching the length of my body. "Right through here."

The female follows and stands next to me. "It's a wall."

"No, it's a portal."

"Is the place it leads to on the ground level?"

"Mmhm."

"So I walk through here, and I arrive elsewhere?"

"Yeah, you could say that."

She glances at me, then hurls herself at the closed portal, smacking her face into the wall.

She bounces back, lands on her bottom, and rubs her forehead.

Most unexpected. "Are you well?"

She's rubbing her forehead and nodding.

"Can your people walk through walls?" I ask.

The female snaps her head up. "No, my people can't walk through walls."

"You slammed into it for what reason, then?"

She throws up her hands. "Gee, Nen, I don't know. I'm trapped in a hole in a mountain with a naked alien male who just told me they use portals to get around, so you bet I tried to walk into one and escape."

My smile is a show of sharp teeth when I crouch before her. "Female, you are nearing heat. I suggest you fix up your nest over there and get comfortable with me soon, because when your heat comes, we will be breeding. For many spans. Now, if you'll excuse me, I need to gather food for those spans, because guess what?" I tap my chest. "I'm extremely eager to hear you beg."

"You're crazy."

"Not yet, but if you refuse me, I can become crazy with need and rut over you. It's best if I didn't."

She chuckles nervously. "We can't breed."

"I assure you we can." The alien is testing me! My teeth are going to shatter if I clench my jaw harder than I have been.

She shakes her head, vehemently. "We're not of the same species."

"Omega and Alpha are the only way Ila and the Omi mate. It seems to me the species is irrelevant, though it helps that I'm attractive and so are you." I stand to my full height so that she may assess my fitness.

Truly testing me, she stares at the floor.

"You are welcome to look, Ila. I'm confident you will find

me fit, and my knot is ready. That's what you came for. To fuck the Omi. Go on, female, take a look."

"You're arrogant."

"I am the Omi." I puff out my chest. "Other predators fear me."

She snaps her head up. "What predators?"

"Land ones."

"There's predators down there?"

Wha... "Of course."

"Holy crap."

"Divine waste can be eliminated in the baths. The water runs and does not recycle back into the baths."

"How the hell did predators get here?"

"We've been here all along."

Silence. The female becomes pale and props her body up with an arm on the floor as if she's feeling faint.

I crouch beside her.

She screams and lashes out, scratching my face, then scurries around the corner, presumably back into her nest.

Communicating with an alien is difficult and confusing, and...I'm leaving to gather food. I hate when goddesses toy with us. Hate it.

CHAPTER SIX

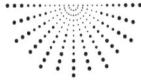

GWEN

*T*he male used "we" when he said predators have been here all along. He is one of the predators, one of the dual-form species our National Security wants to eliminate from the universe because aliens classified as predators predate on humans. How in God's (or goddess's, for that matter) name are they living on Joylius, a planet humanity colonized?

Death by predator is terrible. I've watched the documentaries of jaguars jumping on their prey and the struggle that lasts only minutes but appears to last for eternity while the gazelle tries to escape the jaguar's claws holding her down. He won't let go. He's hungry, and he needs to eat or he'll die.

In the nest, I dress in my old clothes, throwing my underwear out of the nest. I'll wash 'em before using them again. Glancing down my body, I press a hand on my belly and feel the heat churning inside me, even on the skin under my palm. My nipples perk, my breasts start tingling, and my hand trails lower. I touch myself. I'm so wet, two fingers enter easily. I barely feel them. It's almost as if I've expanded down there.

I withdraw my fingers. I don't want to touch my clit. I don't. I touch my bud anyway. Large and swollen, it enjoys my circling it. Swallowing, I moan and lean back in the nest, close my eyes, and rub myself.

As terrible as it sounds, I think about the alien (who is a predator species) and his massive cock and the swollen knot at the base of it. My brain conjures up images of our sweaty bodies. He's mounting me, fucking me so hard, he's pistoning into my small body, and I swear, my pussy channel expands as I rub it, seeking that fat knot that's gonna grow even bigger inside me, blocking the entrance. How do I know this is what it'll do? Oh Lord, everything is wrong here.

I come with a scream, then snap open my eyes, breathing heavily while my pussy spasms. My belly is visibly contracting, and I lift up on my elbows to see clear liquid practically gushing out of my pussy. Gross.

What is happening to me? I lie back down and stare at the light bugs on the ceiling. I pray the male has really left and not lingered, for surely he would have heard me.

I lie there a few minutes, legs spread wide open, liquid trickling out of me. The pain in my belly's gone, though the churning heat hasn't subsided. I touch my stomach, and it's hot, too hot. Maybe I'm getting sick with fever. Yeah, that must be it, not some sort of mating heat or even a mating call for a predatory species.

Jesus, what am I to do?

I'm trapped at the top of a mountain.

I tried escaping and ended up slamming into a wall.

And portals? Who the heck travels via portals? That's the stuff from kids' fantasy books. But the male wasn't joking. The way he said portal seemed as casual as if he was talking about a car. It's normal to him.

Groaning, I stand and put on my shorts, then get up to wash my underwear, wondering why I'm bothering with any clothes. My pussy is leaking, my breasts are heavy with hard nipples, and my skin's sensitive even to my own touch.

I feel like a bitch in heat. "It's fever," I tell myself, not knowing which is worse, heat from wanting to mate or fever from sickness.

A whoosh of air knocks me off my feet, and I plop down. The bird's landed on the platform above the pond. In its beak is a dead animal that he drops on the ground and then proceeds to rip apart using his beak and talons.

I retreat back into the nest.

The male is the bird. At least I think so. He's a predator. A *predator.*

I still can't believe it. For God's sake, this classification is rarely ever mentioned. We know about them, but nobody talks about them. It's as if they don't exist. They do, though. The male said they do. He's standing right around the corner with a dead animal he caught so he can feed me.

Amid the furs, I curl up into a ball and take a few minutes to feel sorry for myself. I'd rather be working at Majestic right now, and that's saying something since the rich and their offspring make some of the worst customers I've ever had the displeasure of serving.

Click click click.

Those are talons scraping the hard ground.

I lift my head.

The bird's red eye peeks around the corner, but this time, his beak extends to the other wall. At the end of it hangs a piece of red meat. My belly rumbles, but I don't sit up. I lie back down. Maybe I'll waste away here in the warm furs. I hear clicking again, and from the corner of my eye, I spot the bird hovering over me.

Blood drips from his beak to my cheek. I wipe it and sit up. Oh girl, his neck is longer than my body. I feel small and helpless, and I don't know what to do.

He steps back and nudges the edge of the nest, then peeps at me.

"I can't eat raw meat." People do sometimes eat raw meat, so I could, possibly, but surely I can somehow conjure up a fire and a pan… Come to think of it, I haven't seen a kitchen, a living room, cutlery, nothing, not even a closet. Where does he get his clothes?

The bird leaves, and I stare at the chunk of beef. I'm gonna call it beef. Filet mignon, which I eat well done, but whatever. My mouth salivates, and before I talk myself out of it, I grab the meat and stuff it into my mouth, then chew. Bile rises, and my belly with it. I force myself to eat the still-warm flesh with blood dripping down my chin.

I step out of the nest so I don't dirty it and stand there with my hand pushing the meat into my mouth so I don't regurgitate.

I manage to swallow some of it, but I can't make myself eat the rest. I spit and go around the corner to wash up.

I collide with his chest. He holds me so I don't fall. I struggle. He won't let go, and his cock is fully erect, the knot a small balloon at the base.

He is nude and male and makes me want to rub myself on his face. He's also a bird of prey that can change forms at will.

A thumb wipes the blood off my chin, and he puts it into his mouth. There's something so mesmerizing about his thumb in his mouth that I press closer. The red of his eyes blazes, matching the color of the molten lava in my belly.

I open my mouth, and for the first time hear myself speak in a language I don't know.

I say, "You may take me now, predator."

Surprised, I widen my eyes.

Nen doesn't react the same way. He's not shocked at all.

He grabs me and picks me up, then slams me against the

wall. That fat cock of his finds my pussy and enters in a single thrust. I gasp, digging my fingernails into his skin as he fucks me, making me hitch breaths and roll my eyes to the back of my head. He feels so good, so right, so satisfying, and I've never felt like this before. His cock is so massive that even my stretched pussy is having a hard time taking it, and the knot at the base of it bumps the outer walls of my pussy, stimulating my anal hole, making me want to beg him to fuck me there too, to mount me, to hold me down and press me against the cold ground.

He ruts over me.

I wrap my fingers around his neck and squeeze. He groans, and I squeeze harder, and Nen slams his mouth over mine. Our teeth clash, tongues intertwine, and the lavalike heat in my belly drops lower, spills, and I swear to God, I feel it coating my channel.

In the back of his throat, Nen growls, as if he can feel my heat too.

He starts pistoning into me.

I peel my mouth away from his to catch my breaths. My breasts slap my skin as they bounce up and down, my orgasm building and building, hovering inside me, heating me up more. Nen's claws dig into my hip, and he throws back his head, exposing his neck to me.

I lean in and bite his throat. The second my teeth close over his skin, Nen roars, a shrieking sound I've only ever heard in fantasy movies with dragons when they spit fire out of their mouths.

Jets of seed gush inside me, and my body convulses, my belly contracts, releasing the pent-up heat from inside me. I bite him harder as tremors rack my body, and I can't stop coming.

Every time his cock jerks, I orgasm.

This goes on for minutes, not seconds, and I hold on to

his body, scratching him, trying to bring him closer, trying to wring every last drop of seed out of him. Our bodies keep contracting. Finally, Nen has the presence of mind to speak, while I can barely form a thought beyond that I want to breed with him like this forever.

"Did you like the terrik?" he asks while still twitching inside me.

I clear my throat and speak in a normal language I hear as English, though I truly believe I'm not speaking it anymore and there're crazy things happening here. "What's a terrik?"

"A small and delicious prey creature. Like you." He licks the side of my neck, then kisses my collarbone.

"It was a good meal," I say.

"*Thank you, Alpha* is in order."

"Thank you, Alpha."

"That's good to hear, Omega. You're learning fast. Your fuck hole made a mess on my cock. Clean it up." Nen puts me down and stands back. His cock drips fluid on the floor. He swipes some with his thumb and eats it first, then smears it over my lips. I taste the fluid we made. It's sweet and spicy, heavy like marmalade, and not like bleach or medical supplies.

"I'm hungry for this." I speak in that language again, and this time, my voice is sultry, smooth, inviting. I sound like a siren lulling this male into carnal pleasures, and before I can think about it, I drop to my knees and proceed to lick him clean.

Above me, Nen rests his palms on the wall, watching me. The red in his eyes disappears behind a solid white membrane, and he says, "I haven't walked in over two turns. But you make me want to never fly as a bird again."

I rise and wipe my mouth.

He grips my throat, and I struggle as he lifts me on my toes. "Ila, hear me. I will not serve you in your heat so you can abandon me and the chicks. I like the human too much to let her go. I am keeping her. So if you came back for the Omi's knot, you're staying with said Omi until the end of our time, not just *your* time." He releases my throat, but only to cage me in with his hands on the wall on either side of my cheeks.

He dips his head, lips touching mine. "Nod your head, Omega."

I do, but mainly because I don't want to piss him off. He's practically declared marriage over here without asking me for my hand. A lifetime spent with him means marriage where I come from. I won't commit to him like that, even though now, after sex, the cramps and the molten lava in my lower belly are gone. I feel much better, and my head isn't so muddied with thoughts of him mounting me.

He pecks my lips. "I will be gone most of the span."

"What? Why?"

He smiles. "Will you miss me?"

"Maybe. I don't want to be alone up here."

"Hm." He appears thoughtful. "I've lived alone up here all my life."

I think of the time I've spent on Joylius and away from my dad and sister and how lonely it gets when you have nobody to tell about your days. As the days roll into months of the high season on Joylius, it gets harder, not easier.

I cup his cheek. "That must've been a lonely life."

He tilts his head. "Is your species highly social? Do they build communities and…talk to others often?"

"Yes."

"We fly solo. We rarely gather, and if we do, it's for something important."

"We gather for no reason at all. We just like seeing each other's faces."

"Will you miss that about your people?"

"I'm still hoping I'll see my people someday."

Nen nods. "I will bring you other people. From the village. You can look at their faces for as long as you please. After your heat. Speaking of heat, it has started rather abruptly, and I need to hunt and gather for the duration of it since I'll be mostly with you in the nest."

"This is all so very animalistic and strange for me. I'm going to need a moment or a year to process what's happening to me. Us. The heat. The fact that you're a bird."

"The bird is unimportant right now. What is important is that Ila breeds with the Omi. I am the Omi, an Alpha to your Omega. Ila has only bred three times in recorded history."

He points at the wall, and I turn. His claw traces the scriptures. "Ila could not conceive with land predators. She developed unexplained fevers, and Bera grew worried her daughter would die. One evening, Bera found Ila sneaking away with a bird of prey instead of a land predator. When Ila returned home, Bera left to pay the male a visit. She gifted him a knot that could swell and become cold inside Ila so Ila wasn't uncomfortable in her heat. When the knot swelled and the female was seeded, the Omi bonded Ila. Such a bond was unique to the pair of them. Bera made him an Alpha to Ila's Omega so that she could breed with the predator she most desired."

As Nen read the words, the scribbling turned into letters, and in my head, I can now connect them and make sense of them. "What is all this?"

"Old scriptures." Nen throws a hand over my shoulder and pulls us back so we can view the entire wall.

"Who wrote those?" I ask.

"Bera did. This nest is a shrine, the most fertile place in the land. She wanted Ila to have whatever her heart desired, and when Ila couldn't conceive, Bera took matters into her own hands."

A vision of a female appears on the wall. I swallow. "Do you see her?" I whisper.

"I do not. What do you see?"

"A woman holding on to a rope suspended from the ceiling, a paintbrush in her hand. The walls are darker than they are now, and she's painting. No, writing in light blue ink. She's left-handed. Like me." I chuckle nervously.

"What does she look like?" He shudders, claws scratching his belly.

"The woman is taller than me. Long straight black hair reaching the back of her knees. Her tanned skin is darker than mine, and she's more voluptuous, her hips fanning out in an almost impossible way." The woman's brush hand halts, and she turns her profile as if listening to us.

This is scary. My heart's beating like a rabbit's.

Before she glances over her shoulder, I know she'll turn. I know she'll see me, and I know this from memory. This moment in time happened before. I stood here, in this place, and walked in on my mother writing on the wall right above the place I mated an Omi.

My heart beats wildly. I grab Nen's forearm and move closer to him. I know her. I would know her anywhere.

My mother slowly turns her head and looks right at me. Her eyes are white, the same color that Nen's are now.

The vision disappears, but I keep staring at the wall. "I know why Ila chose me."

"You believe me now. This is good. Blessed Bera. We will pay homage to her."

"I believe what I saw. A woman with whom I shared a memory. I can't explain it any other way. Science would say I'm crazy."

"You are not. Goddess Amti presides over madness and lust."

"Maybe I'm Amti? Conjuring up visions."

47

"Amti is not an Omega. You're an Omega. Tell me, why did Ila chose you?"

"I paint letters. Elegant letters that look beautiful on canvas."

"It is set, then," Nen says and turns to me. "While I hunt and gather, you will paint letters."

My heart leaps at the prospect of painting an entire wall and doing that for days, completely losing track of time and people. Solitude while painting is most welcome. I guess we're not always in need of socializing either. Sometimes our passions take over, and we do more of what we love doing. And I love calligraphy. "Where can I find paint?"

Nen scratches his head and shakes out his shoulders. "I do not know. I'll search the other room."

"Oh, there's another room?"

"There are many rooms."

"Where?"

He shakes his head. "I will show you some other time."

"Why not now?"

"The bird is very messy."

He talks about the bird in third person now. That's funny. I chuckle. "I doubt it's messier than me and my closet."

"Hmm, you will also need clothes." Nen walks away mumbling, and that's when I see the stairs leading to the platform.

"There're stairs," I shout after him.

"I know," he shouts back.

"Where did they come from?"

"The portal that hides stuff I don't need. Stairs are one of them."

"Thank you!" I shout and climb the stairs, intent on searching for the other room.

CHAPTER SEVEN

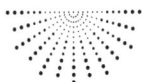

GWEN

*T*he hallway leading out of the nest space is a large tunnel, large enough for the bird to fit through. I'm still not quite at ease knowing Nen is actually a predatory species but I am okay for as long as he's not hurting me.

He fucked me. He fucked me so good that I'm sore between my legs and feeling like I want more of him and soon. Heat in my belly slowly returns, and I try not to think about him or his body.

It's not even the body. His touch and how he looks at me, as if I hung the moon, makes me all warm inside, and not just in a heated way. I don't know a single guy who looked at me that way or any dudes who would worship the female as a goddess.

Nen worships the female. An Omega. Ila is his woman, and I am her, apparently. I can't explain the heat, the language, or the vision of a woman I know is my mother. She seemed nice, and her smile was warm. The story about her made me feel like I belong.

My real mother dropped me off on Dad's doorstep. She came in and out of my life like wind. Sometimes she would storm into the house, declaring everlasting love so that Dad would give her one more chance. Every time he did, my sister and I knew she was playing him.

Daddy is a good man who believes in the family unit, and even though he doesn't love her, he loves the idea of us having a mother. If I am to stay with Nen, I will miss him.

Perhaps as I get to know Nen better, I could ask him to take me to mainland Joylius so I could at least call my dad and tell him not to worry. I don't know how in God's (or the goddess's) name predators live on this planet and how National Security hasn't found them, or maybe they found them and aren't telling the rest of humanity.

The tunnel's nearing an end, and I pause to watch Nen on the edge of the platform, just standing there looking perfectly comfortable on the Mount Everest of Joylius. He turns as if he knows I'm watching. Nen spreads his arms and lets his body fall. I slap a hand over my mouth and wait.

A great big bird comes swooping up. It bats its wings and pummels wind toward me as he whistles.

Oh, what the hell. I whistle back.

Nen disappears under the mountain. Lingering, I wonder if I'll ever get to see him transform from man to bird and confirm this predator thing with my own two eyes.

I rest my hand on the wall, then feel a corner. I peer around it. I can't see much in the dark space, but I think I can make out a room.

When I step inside, the odor assaults me, and I grab the collar of my shirt and pull it over my nose. It smells stale in here and reminds me of abandoned basements with mold and bird crap everywhere. Does the bird crap in here?

Oh Lord, I need to stop thinking.

Walking around, I keep my hand on the wall because I can't see and don't want to venture blindly inside. I trip over something and nearly fall. Why are there no bugs in here?

I need the light. Gotta go get some bugs. Ew.

Back in the nest, I stand before the wall, thinking of grabbing some bugs to take with me, but I really hate bugs. I hate insects in general. I glance at the nest and pick up a huge red pelt. It kind of reminds me of those animals that stalked my pod. No, wait. Those are all predators. Is this what I think it is?

I spread out the pelt and walk around it. Oh yes, this pelt once belonged to one of them. I can make out the shape of the animal. Predators really are what we think they are. Vicious. They make bedding out of their own people.

I return it to the nest and grab my clean underwear and use it to scoop up some bugs.

Back in the other room, I place the bugs on the wall, and to my delight, they latch onto the surface immediately, one on top of the other. I frown. I think they're multiplying. They're having sex and insta-multiplying, and soon enough, the entire side of the wall is lit up. They're spreading over the room so quickly that I only have to wait a few minutes to see. And boy, do I see what Nen means by the "bird is very messy."

The bird stacked piles upon piles of random objects in all four corners of the room. Clothes, weapons, shields, bowls, and even old bones and skulls I can't quite classify as any animal I know. Dry flowers decorate a large skull mounted on a wall. I recognize it as another bird of prey, perhaps someone important to Nen. Important enough to be remembered.

I walk to a shallow hole in the ground and pick up a metal stick. Or try to. I can't lift it. I'm pretty sure it's a fire poker. I could start a fire here and fry the meat I need to eat. As I explore the room, I'm careful where I step, avoiding the bones littering the ground.

There're clothes piled up near one corner, and I pick up

the first thing that draws my eye. A red pelt, but this one sewn as a throw. I shrug it over my shoulders and look down my body. Definitely a winter coat.

I grab another pelt, a silver-gray one. Soft. Oh man, really soft. I reach for more like it and find three, then turn to carry them to the nest.

A shadow stands at the entrance.

I scream and drop the pelts.

The shadow retreats.

"Nen?" I call out, then scoop up one pelt and shake the dirt from it.

He doesn't answer.

I whistle.

He whistles back.

"You scared the crap out of me." I get the other two pelts and shake them out too. "Next time, please announce yourself. Some of us humans are faint of heart. Anyway, I found the spare room. Hope you don't mind. I'm looking for paint." I picked up pelts, it seems. Oh well.

Nen's covered in darkness, keeping inside the tunnel and not stepping into the lit room. The outline of his body seems smaller, though no less than six three, so that's saying something. I don't think this is Nen. I grip the pelt as if it's a shield.

"Who are you?" I ask.

He clears his throat. "Diwi."

"Diwi, I'm…" I hesitate. If I am a goddess, would he fear me? If I'm a human, would he eat me? "Nen left to hunt and gather. He will return shortly."

"I know."

"Then you know you shouldn't be here."

"How would I know that?"

Um, good point.

He continues. "You called me. I was not going to speak with you."

"I didn't call you."

He whistles.

"That was when I thought you were Nen."

"Nevertheless, you called. What are you, female?"

He asked *what*, not *who*, but I'm going with who and he can deduce the what. "Ila. My name is Ila."

The male is still and remains hidden in the shadows, but what I wouldn't give to see his facial expression or even his body language now.

"Ila," he repeats.

"That's right."

"Impossible."

He echoes my thoughts, and yet deep down inside, I know it to be true. I have snippets of memories that aren't mine and aren't Earthy. If I reach for them, think about them, explore them, allow them to form more, I bet I would see myself flying on the wind. Which is crazy, so I'm not doing it.

"Nen said I'm Ila," I tell him.

"He's gone insane with solitude, and he's imagining things. You are food." The male steps toward me.

"Stay where you are."

"I don't think so."

I backpedal, and he pursues, coming into the light. He's tall, dark, and handsome with a masculine nose that slightly curves down. He's built like someone carved him out of a mountain. Large and imposing, but not as large as Nen. Every step I take back, he takes forward. Stopping for a second, he flares his nostrils. His eyelids flutter, and he sticks his tongue out as if tasting the air.

I fling the pelt over his head and make a beeline toward the nest. Pumping my legs and arms as fast as I can, I almost slide down the steps. Deep male laughter follows me.

"The thrill is in the hunt, prey."

I step behind the corner and peek at the platform. He's standing there, blazing red eyes locked with mine as I peek around the wall. The predator bends at the knees and jumps over the bath, materializing before me in a split second. He grabs me by my shoulders and presses his body against mine.

My back hits the wall. Between his legs, he's hard. "The combined scents of an Omega in heat and prey to be consumed is something I've never encountered. If you are a goddess, then lust and madness is your power. Amti," he chants. "Sweet Amti."

Where are my godly powers now? I don't have any, so I make a fist and punch him in the throat. Pain spreads over my knuckles, and I yelp.

He grunts and takes my wrists, then secures them above my head. His face is inches from mine, and his eyes blaze with lust. "Amti," he repeats, and slams his mouth on mine. Freezing cold air rushes out of my lungs and into his mouth.

The male rears back and grabs his throat, gasping for air, his eyes wide, the red in them dimming until they're white. Webs of tiny blood vessels show on his face and turn blue as if his blood is turning to ice. He runs past me, and I turn to watch him leap over the pond and land on two feet while his upper body grows, arms turn into wings, and his head becomes that of an Om bird of prey.

It is one thing to know and be told these males are predators, but a whole different experience to watch the transformation happen before your eyes. The male is gone in a flash.

I breathe a sigh of relief and note my breath fogs the air like on a winter morning. Except it's cold in a warm place. I grew up in New Jersey, so I've had an opportunity to walk outside my house when the first snow comes for Christmas and blow out hot breaths. I pretend I'm there now.

I inhale a lungful and bend to blow, like some sort of

dragon spitting fire. A gust of freezing white air rushes out of me and reaches the pond, then spreads over it, lifting the water, making a wave. The water splashes back down, and I do it again. This time, I freeze a path across the pond.

"Well, this is cool."

The ice over the water melts almost instantly but I could do this all day. If I had a day, and I don't. The nest is messy. Turning back toward the nest, I stare at it, unhappy with how it's arranged. It's soft but could be softer, fluffier. There needs to be a small space for me in the corner of it where I can curl up. I need those pelts. Returning to the other room, I grab the pelts and head back, stopping before I exit. The hallway is dark and ominous, and other predators will soon find out about me.

I fist the pelts and curb my fear, but still peek into the hallway before I step outside.

CHAPTER EIGHT

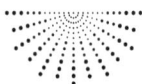

NEN

I caught not one but two terriks for my Omega. Terriks are small and fast little fuckers with excellent hearing. They're hard for us to catch because by the time I'm diving after it, most of them hear me plummeting through the air. They dig a hole and hide inside, and unless I dig too, I fly over it and on to the next prey. I hate digging. Dirt gets under my talons and annoys me. Besides, I leave the digging to land predators. They like rolling in the dirt. I'm a clean bird. I bathe daily.

She liked the first one and will like these chubby ones even better. The chubby ones have fat, and they taste sweeter. But since the terriks are small and don't do much for sating my hunger in a normal span, let alone during the mating when my body loses fluids and produces the Omega marking scents Ila needs for my seed to take inside her womb, I need to return for a night hunt.

Most small prey hide at night. Larger prey who predate on the smaller ones come out for hunting, so I can have a proper meal and gather up one or two to take back to the nest.

Dropping the terriks on the platform, I land on two feet, practicing a swift transformation at the same time. Two feet are so awkward looking. I stare at them, wiggling one foot before picking up the terrik and taking it inside. For a change, I'll clean up the terriks with a knife instead of my beak. I honestly wonder if I can still remember how to prep food using my hands.

With a chuckle, I enter the nest and even use the stairs, rounding the corner to find Ila facing the wall and...levitating. I develop an itch on my thigh, shoulders, back of my neck. The image of her hovering in the air unsettles me.

"Brought terriks again. Three in one day," I say, my voice steady despite the discomfort I feel.

"Omega," I call out.

Ila startles and falls into the nest, then scrambles to get up and smiles at me. But she doesn't smile as if she's happy to see me. It's... It's...the kind of smile that makes me want to fuck her for a cycle. Ila crawls the length of the nest, her hair hanging down on one side, her breasts swaying.

I drop the terriks and turn away to go take a dip inside the bath before I touch her. Fuck! Cold cold cold. I leap out. "What happened to the baths?" I ask, coming back to the nest.

Ila sits in the middle of the nest, long eyelashes framing pretty, almost entirely black eyes. Her pupils are dilated. The scent of Omega heat drifts to me, and my cock hardens instantly, my knot starting to inflate.

"You're ready for me," I say.

"I am."

"Did you nest?"

"I have."

"Where did you get those extra pelts?" I approach the nest and stand over her. She places her palms on my thighs. Her mouth opens and closes over the tip of my dick. Her back is lovely and ends in generous buttocks that flare out as she kneels. The sight and smell of a goddess Omega make me forget about the nest or pelts or my entire life, for that matter, and all I want to do is have her suck my cock.

Goddesses are beautiful, terrifying creatures who use up males and discard them. While Ila desires the Omi and can only breed with the Omi, she is a goddess of desire and can draw any male to her. During her heat, she is the most vulnerable and, scriptures say, unable to manipulate winds, only desire. Desire for the Omi, and for her Omi to desire her back.

My people have written that a union of the Omi and Ila is felt across the lands, that it fuels Bera's fertility, and as Ila's mouth warms my cock and I stroke her hair, I wonder if Om females will enter their own heats. Unlike most tribes, we still have some females. But they haven't been entering heats as they should, and so my males can't breed them.

"Omega, your mouth feels wonderful."

The brown of her eyes is almost all gone now, her scent potent and strong, luring me into the nest. I step forward and sink my cock deeper down her throat. Ila doesn't choke. Her throat makes room for my cock, and I grab her cheeks and slowly fuck her throat until she taps my thigh, telling me she's out of air. I pull back and wait a few moments while the tip dribbles my seed onto her tongue.

Ila swallows it.

"Are you hungry for more seed?" I murmur.

She nods, and I push inside her mouth, cupping her cheeks as I guide my cock down her throat. Ila's eyes widen, and tears cloud them. I fuck her mouth, depositing precum seed inside it with each thrust so it can land in her hungry belly. Pausing when I almost come, I slap her cheeks, first one, then the other.

Ila groans and digs her blunt fingernails into my thigh.

"Do you know what I like about you most?"

She shakes her head, cheeks a bright red.

"You're prey. Blunt teeth, no claws. Everything about you is cute, submissive, and fuckable." I take my cock out and tap her nose with it. She pouts, then tries to put it back into her mouth.

I crouch in front of the nest, then grab her throat and squeeze. My cum slides out and lingers at the corner of her mouth. I kiss both her cheeks, feeling how warm they are from my slaps, then lick my seed from the edges of her lips. "Mmm, I taste yummy."

Ila nods and sits back on her heels. Her hands rest on her thighs so her generous breasts are pushed together. I dip a finger between her breasts and move it back and forth. "There's not a single part of your body that I don't wanna fuck. Breasts, mouth, even your toes."

Ila's rising, trying to stick her nipples into my mouth. When I don't take them, she lifts one breast and rubs a nipple over my lips, practically begging.

"Why are your nipples not leaking yet? Let's make them leak." I squeeze her breasts, and a tiny drop of clear fluid comes out of the nipple.

Ila looks down and then up at me, her face bright red. "Oh my God," she whispers.

I wipe another tiny drop from her breast and smear it over my lips. "Come here and taste Bera's nectar."

Ila shakes her head, huffs out a breath, and looks away. She trails one hand between her legs and touches herself, then pulls back. "I feel like an animal in heat."

"You are a goddess in heat."

"What's the difference?"

I lean in and kiss the top of her breast. I want to squeeze it and suck the nectar right out, but I won't because these breasts are going to fill and grow, and when our chicks hatch, they'll need it. Land predators wonder why Om are so large. We are large because of genetics and a long line of strict tribal breeding.

Om breeds with Om, and as long as we breed with each other, Bera provides our females with the nectar that makes us larger and stronger, placing us at the very top of the food chain.

I suck on her nipple, drawing it out, and get a drop. I can't resist. The nectar is sweet, and my teeth ache for more, and I want to suck and fuck Ila till the end of our time. She's an addiction, and I'll never sate it.

Ila grabs my cock, and I detach from her breast, then shake my head.

I can't forget she's the goddess of desire, and my needs are heightened around her.

She strokes me slowly with one hand, dipping the fingers of the other hand into her pussy. She fucks herself with them, and I watch, waiting for her face to heat up, for her mouth to open, for her to start coming.

"No." I grab her wrist before she makes herself come. I lick her fingers, bite one gently, and suck on them.

When I release her arm, she slaps me the way I slapped her.

My cock spurts into her hand and my balls tighten, readying the seed to flood. My body's gonna burst.

Ila removes her hand. A cramp hits my balls and makes me kneel, almost folding over.

Ila smirks. "I will have all that I desire, predator."

I grab her throat and squeeze again. "You will have it when I'm good and ready to give it to you. Now, stop teasing me and invite me into your nest."

Ila smiles. "I want to come."

I slap her breast. "No."

A cold breeze ruffles my hair. I take it as a threat. Ila's

angry that I'm denying her. I lean in and whisper at her ear, "If you hit me with the wind, you will lose the privilege of my fat knot and spend the rest of your heat in agony, a begging, slobbering mess."

"You wouldn't."

"I would." We lock eyes. It's a battle of wills. Ila's a goddess. I'm her Alpha male. I can't allow her to threaten me with wind when she doesn't get what she wants. "You will come when I let you come, Ila. The nest?" I prompt.

"Okay," she says, and when I release her, she lies back and spreads her legs, her pussy on full display for me. I stride into the nest like a bird conqueror. Soft pelts cushion my feet and the lights dim down, throwing my large shadow over her small body.

Omega honey leaks out of her pussy. It is the prettiest sight my eyes have ever seen, and I've seen many beautiful things from above.

I extend a hand, and Ila takes it. I help her up and turn her by the shoulders, then place my palm between her shoulder blades, encouraging her to bend slightly. She rests her palms on the wall, keeping her legs pressed together, teasing me, making me have to work to reach her pussy.

I fist my cock and rest it on her ass and give my knot a squeeze, shooting a bit of seed onto the small of her back. It trails down between her ass cheeks. Ila sighs, the seed a cool balm against her heated skin.

I stand at her side, one finger following the path of my seed. At the tip of my finger, I feel a dip. I poke it. Ila's head snaps up and turns my way. Her eyes are all pupils and dilated now, black like midnight, no brown to be found. I enjoy how it contrasts against the white. "Two fuck holes." I kiss her shoulder. "Blessed be the span you crashed into the river."

I coat my finger with seed, then dip it inside the small

tight fuck hole, watching Ila for reaction. She shudders and pushes back, dipping my finger inside her more. This hole grips my finger so tightly that I groan when I think of what it's gonna do when I stretch it with my cock.

But for now, I remove my finger in favor of my thumb stroking her pussy hole. It's wide, and when I shove my thumb inside, it spasms around it. "Your pussy is ready to take the knot. It's so ready that I can stick my fist inside your greedy pussy."

Ila moans.

"Shall I?"

She shakes her head.

I snort. "You want the knot." I stroke her and place the palm of my other hand on her belly, gently press on it. Liquid gushes onto my other hand.

"Oh God, what are you doing to me?"

"Whatever I want. In heat, you're at my mercy, and I will take your submission and wanton desire as far as I please. When I'm done with you, you will be a puddle of liquid desire, melting in your nest, unable to lift a single finger. But don't worry, I'll keep going and fucking you even when you want to rest. I'll fuck you for as long as I'm able. And female, I'm fit and able."

I stroke her hole and the swollen bud at the top of her entrance. I don't know why humans come with the bud, but Ila moans and begs for the knot when I stroke the little thing. I dance my fingers over it, and I keep pressing her belly, forcing the liquid to gush out of her channel.

Ila's blunt fingernails scrape the wall and her knees start to shake. She finally spreads her legs.

I slap her pussy.

She screams.

I move around her and kneel to open my mouth. Omega honey drips onto my tongue, and my eyes roll to the back of my head. Sweetness straight from the source. I close the distance and kiss the small lips there, tilting my head, then spread her ass cheeks so I can make out with her pussy like I would with her mouth.

Ila sits back on my face and grinds her ass onto me, gushing liquid on my tongue. I'm greedy for it, horny for it, my balls hanging heavy below my cock.

I palm them and rub them gently, then spurt cum on her leg while the Omega moans, her pussy spasming. She's coming and coming, leaking fluid all over my mouth and beard.

Standing, I wipe my beard and smear her juice on her back.

"What a mess you make."

I grab her hip with one hand and under her belly with the other and lift a little while I bend at the knees. From behind, I enter her and exhale a breath at the same time as my cock spurts semen inside her, and Ila hangs her head.

"You feel so good," she tells me. "Ice to the fire inside me."

My seed cools her heat so she feels better and not so feverish, which in turn tames her desires. If she's gonna use her desire on me, it's a risky game, since I also secretly desire to consume her. I might never get over that desire, but at least I can control it, know she's Ila, and become used to the scent of both prey and Omega. A breeder meant to breed only with me.

I slowly slide in and out of her, pressing her belly with my palm so that I'm also milking her liquid. I feel the heat flush down my cock, preparing her pussy for when I want to fuck her with the knot.

Ila's pussy won't tear when the knot enters, and I can fuck her with my knot inflated. The knot is not used while fucking, only after. An Omega female would tear if the inflated knot was withdrawn from inside her.

But I can fuck Ila any way I want, and blessed be Ila, for she provokes my darkest desires. Ones that make me slap her ass cheeks, grab her hair, fist it, yank her to me, and push my cock inside her to the start of the knot. "You want the knot?"

She nods.

I slap her cheek.

She slaps me back.

Oh Bera, mother of all, how I love thee for birthing this creature. I snarl and snap my teeth near her ear, then press her against the wall and fuck her hard until I come and the knot inflates.

Ila's murmuring things I can't understand. My knot blows up inside her, and she sighs, relieved by the chill of it. A shiver runs down her body. I start slowly withdrawing my cock. Her pussy stretches over the fat knot as I'm pulling back, looking down so I can see what it looks like. Fluid coats my knot, which is halfway out of her.

I withdraw all the way, then start pushing back in, noting the small fuck hole expanding too. It wants something. I give it my thumb and fuck that hole too while moving Ila's Omega pussy over my knot, taking care I don't go into a frenzy and pound her now.

Ila's moans tell me she's enjoying this, but she can't stand anymore. She's sliding down the wall, and I have to hold her up if I wanna fuck her like this.

I pick her up and let her kneel, face on the furs, arms spread out, eyes closed. She's done. I'm not. I am so not. Moving in and out of her, I say, "I've waited my entire life for you." I push my thumb back into her small fuck hole. I'm really liking the grip this hole has on it. "And I'm never letting you go."

CHAPTER NINE

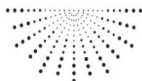

GWEN

*I*n the movies, when lovers finish up their night, the woman always ends up with her cheek resting on the man's chest or at least she wakes up that way. He strokes her hair and back as he's gazing down on her sleeping. That's how humans do it in the movies.

The Omi does not.

The Omi fucked me for what seemed like hours before he emptied inside me, and I came at least four times that I can count, though if I'm being honest, Ila (that's me) spent the entire time coming, the liquid gushing out of her without control or mercy for my human side and the embarrassment I felt when I realized I was leaking even from my breasts. I don't know if I can look Nen in the eyes, so it's a good thing he's spooning me.

After he emptied, his inflated knot remained inside me, and my pussy clamped around it, and now we're stuck, much like a pair of dogs in heat. I am definitely some sort of animal. I can never go back to Earth with what I experienced here. Who can possibly sate me there when I'm like this? Nobody. Men aren't made to please me.

Nen forced my body into a ball, with his cocooning mine. His breaths tickle my face as he moves stray hairs from my neck. He buries his nose there and inhales, then bites. "You may rest for a few moments."

I chuckle. "Or a year."

"No, not an entire turn."

I smile. Humor is lost on him. I want to tell him about the male who entered the nest while Nen was gone, but I can't right now. This moment feels secret somehow. Even the walls pulse, pale blue letters lifting up in random places like leaves on a gentle wind. I truly am in the presence of something greater than myself and the alien with me.

"I'm not on Joylius, am I?" It's not a question anymore. I've simply ignored my gut when it screamed at me, telling me this isn't Kansas.

"You are not."

I swallow, heart picking up beats. "Nobody at home knows where I am."

"Nomra Prime is uncharted. We have advanced defenses aimed at keeping intruders away."

"My dad and my sister will worry." Tears roll down my nose and cheeks, and I can't suppress a sob. I press my hand over my mouth, and Nen squeezes me tighter in his arms.

"Don't despair. This is where you belong."

"I don't know that."

"Ila knows."

"But I'm Gwen."

Nen pauses, then asks, "Do your people not have faith in anything beyond themselves?"

"We have one god."

"What?" He releases me, leaving me bare. I grip his wrist and put his arm back around my shoulders while scooting back toward his body. I want to live inside him. He's... my security blanket.

"Mmhm. One God, the Father."

"You worship a male?"

I chuckle. "In a way, yes."

"You can worship me anytime."

Smiling, I twist my upper body to lie on my back and look up at him. His dark hair falls over one broad shoulder, and I take a strand and play with it. It's coarse and thick, rough, unrefined, like a diamond in the rough. "How old are you?" I ask.

"I'm old."

"How old?"

"Old."

"I'm thirty-five," I offer.

"You're ancient," he says.

"Thank you, Nen," I deadpan. "That's real charming."

"Welcome."

I laugh because humor and sarcasm are lost on him. "How old?" I press.

His eyes are white and difficult to read. "Forty-seven turns this coming warm season."

"Not old."

"Spending a lifetime in solitude makes me feel older. Ancient. Though, not as ancient as you."

"Ila, you mean."

He grinds his jaw, and I palm it. I feel his annoyance and self-correct. "I am ancient." Like an old soul. Not *like* an old soul. "I'm an old soul."

Nen nods. "Who rides the winds and indulges our desires. Soon after the heat, pilgrims will start ascending, making their way up to the nest. We must prepare for this before you lay eggs, because after you do, nobody is allowed up here."

Lay eggs? "I can't lay eggs."

"Sure you can."

"I may have babies, but I can't lay eggs."

67

"Sure you can," he repeats.

I shake my head and snap, "I'm not laying eggs, Nen."

His eyes narrow. "Is there something wrong with laying eggs?"

"For a bird, no. For a human, yes."

"Well then, human, you shall become a bird." Nen lies on his back, and because we're still connected, neither of us can pull away. The knot forces intimacy. We should care for each other after the sex craze and argue about the eggs later.

"I don't mean to offend you," I say.

He glares.

"I really don't."

Nen squeezes my hip, and the knot deflates. He detaches from me and begins to get up to leave.

I push at his chest and straddle him. "Where are you going, predator?" My voice is curt, the language ancient.

"You were becoming hostile toward the chicks, which is a great offense both toward me and toward Bera, who blessed you with conceiving with the Omi. She is a goddess of war as well, so you and I, Omega, can either reproduce or go to war. I desire you. I know you can tell, and I don't need to be God to know you desire me. I suggest you stop denying who you've become."

I rest my elbows on his chest and lean in to kiss him on the mouth. "I'm sorry I offended you."

"And Bera."

"And my mother." Ila is a goddess, and she is me, and if I align with her, accept her, I will survive and won't be so freaked out anymore. It's easier said than done, but I can't hold on to my humanity when I'm surrounded by predators.

Nen circles my hip with his claw, sending shivers down my spine. My core starts heating up again. Oh boy. I lick his bottom lip, and he captures my tongue and sucks on it. We kiss like men and women, like humans do, with lazy, slow tongue movements while my Alpha strokes my hip and bottom. My hair curtains his face, and his eyes keep changing from red to white.

"Why do your eyes change color?" I ask.

"The bird's eye is red. White is for male predators. When a male spends too long as a bird, he becomes feral, forgets how to walk or even talk, so I'm having to adjust."

"I'd never have guessed you're adjusting." Because I've been self-centered on my own issues. Ouch. Now that I know he's adjusting as well, perhaps we can adjust together. "How long have you spent in bird form?"

"Two turns."

Two years.

Nen spreads my ass cheeks and traces the outer edges of my butthole, circling it with a claw. My channel contracts, and I rub my breasts on his chest. His beautiful, hard cock nestled between our bodies makes me want to fuck him again. "Take me again," I say, and slide up over his cock and position the tip at my entrance so that when I slide down the Alpha's body, his cock fills me.

Sighing, I close my eyes and sit on him fully. Lifting up with my palms on his chest, I ride his cock. Nen sits up so my breasts rub against his chest, creating friction for my nipples. He lifts my breast and takes it into his mouth, then sucks on it, groaning. His cock spurts precum inside me, cooling my channel while the heat in my belly churns and churns.

"Your body is begging for my seed," he says.

In a frenzy, I pick up my pace and ride him hard and fast.

My vision blurs. I can barely make out his face as I hop up and down on his cock, my breasts bouncing, my hair whipping around my shoulders.

The knot becomes hard again, and I sit on it, making my pussy stretch around it.

Nen grips my throat.

I try moving up and down, but he's holding me. "No." He denies me the knot.

I try sitting on it again and snarl when he holds me.

"You will tear. I will prep you again. At my pace, not yours." He flips us over and settles between my legs, pushing into me slowly. Once I'm impaled to the hilt, he sneaks a hand under my body and pushes a finger into my asshole. I groan, arch my back, and throw my arms above my head and grip the furs as he fucks me slowly, sometimes sitting back on his heels so he can watch his knot coming in and out of me and I can watch his abdomen contract with the effort.

Nen is a sight to behold, his body a perfection of tanned, rock-hard muscle. He's the sexiest male I've ever seen. "You're perfect," I whisper.

He snaps his gaze up. I didn't mean for him to hear that.

"Thank you, Omega. As are you."

CHAPTER TEN

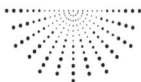

GWEN

*D*uring the heat, we fucked. Even eating, sleeping, and bathing was optional for us. As the days rolled into nights and nights rolled into days, I lost track of time, enjoying myself plenty with Nen in the nest and on top of the furs.

Now that the heat in my belly is gone, my body aches in places that make me wobble as I follow Nen through the dark hallway and out on the platform.

I shield my eyes from daylight and see Nen's doing the same.

"Everything looks as I left it. Let's go back inside," he says.

He's practicing humor.

I smile and give him a thumbs-up.

Sighing, he rests his fists on his hips and bows his head.

"What is it?" I ask.

He snorts. "I don't feel like flying." He looks up and laughs. "I don't feel like flying," he shouts.

I remain quiet. I don't know what to say. I can't even imagine what it's like to have two shapes.

Nen scrubs his face. "But I have to feed us."

"We still have two fish left in the pond." We ate the rest. I tried telling Nen they're like pets and we shouldn't eat them, but he said he eats pets for breakfast, and when I'm hungry, I should too.

I explained about cats and dogs, but I don't think he understands what "pet" means.

He couldn't leave me while I was in heat, and because the heat came on so suddenly, he didn't have time to hunt and gather. Nen is a provider at his core, so not gathering food when we needed it most made him feel bad.

Therefore, I ate the fish sushi style.

"Stay inside," he says.

"It's not like I can leave your cave."

"Having you trapped makes me happy."

"I'm happy to oblige."

"Sarcasm?" he asks.

"Yes."

"It's annoying."

"You'll come to like it."

He smiles. "I'm sure I will." The way he looks at me makes my chest all fluttery and full, and I think maybe I like him much more than I care to admit.

During the heat, he took care of me in every sense of the word, and gained my trust and affection in the process. Maybe it's the same for him, but I won't be the one saying the words first for fear of not hearing them back.

Nen cups my cheeks. "Hear me, because this is important. This mountain is yours, and you can leave the nest at any time. You command the winds."

"How?"

"I wouldn't know how goddesses do anything. They just do it."

"Very helpful."

His eyes narrow. "I'm serious. Listen."

"I'm listening."

"Really?"

"I swear it."

Nen nods. "You are a human female. A prey creature. Beware of predators. When you step outside, and I ask that you don't until I return, instead of looking down and fearing the heights, look up and scan the skies."

"Got it."

"How is your eyesight?"

"Twenty-twenty."

Nen stares blankly.

"It's excellent," I clarify.

"I would like to test your sight and ensure it is at my standard of excellence."

"Okay." I nod.

"There's a predator cruising the skies right now. Point him out to me."

Looking up, I don't see a bird, so I walk farther out onto the platform to stop in the middle and turn in circles, shielding my eyes from the sun. "I don't see anything."

"Oh, my poor human. It is as I feared."

"What is?"

"A predator will lure you into a trap. When you see a flash of blue in a perfectly white or even dark gray cloud, you shouldn't leave your cover to investigate so you can see better. We're designed to not be seen."

"Blue flashing in the sky are the blue feathers under your wings?"

He nods. "They blend with the sky so when prey looks up, we're hard to spot, and when spotted, prey tends to stop to assure themselves they're seeing what they think they're seeing. It is very strange behavior from my perspective, but it is how most prey behaves. Now, I will leave for a few moments. On my way back, you will lift your arm when you first spot me, so I know how far you can see."

"Got it. When I see you, I lift my arm. Should I wave or something?"

He blinks. "Waving is optional."

I clear my throat when my belly rumbles. "How long before you return?"

He traces a claw over my cheek. "Longer than necessary if you will miss me and grow desperate for me."

"Make it short so I don't get hungry and eat you, bird. On Earth, we predate on turkeys, you know."

Nen laughs as he walks backward to the edge of the platform. He spreads his arms, balancing on the brink like a swimmer readying to execute a backflip from the springboard. The height and his standing on the edge of the mountain make me nervous. I bite my nail. "Why do you have to stand there? Can't you stand here and bird up?"

"Are you worried I might fall?" He pinwheels his arms about him, pretending to fall dramatically.

The sound of his bones shifting startles me. Arms extend and become wings, and a moment later, there stands my bird, one red eye on me, head tilted to the side as if trying to see me better.

This is incredible. I don't believe I'll ever get used to seeing the transformation of a dual-form alien.

Nen takes flight, batting his massive wings furiously toward the sun. It takes only a minute before he disappears from view. Carefully scanning the skies, I walk around the platform. Something blue flashes in a single cloud hovering right above me.

"Over here!" I shout and wave my arms. "I see you!"

The bird plummets, red beak and eyes coming into view, and it's gunning right for me. I keep waving. "Definitely see you now."

The bird's almost at me when something black hits it.

The bird shrieks in pain and tumbles in a fury of feathers.

Oh no! I rush to the edge to peek below. Two beaks and four wings tangled in a ball are screeching and tearing each other apart. This is another predator. I bet he's come for food, and I also bet Nen won't let him eat me.

"Stop it!" I scream at the top of my lungs.

A gust of wind comes out of nowhere and slams the birds into the mountain hundreds of feet below me. Their bodies tumble, heads hitting the rocks, wings breaking until they lie belly up.

"Nen," I shout. "Oh no. Oh no." I run to the edge of the platform and stop.

Is he dead? My lungs cease working, and I struggle to breathe.

I can't reach him. I don't know what to do. What do I do?

CHAPTER ELEVEN

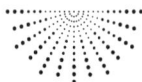

NEN

*K*eeping an eye on my brother, I will my broken body to repair faster. His wing is twisted, and his left leg shattered when he tried to break the fall, but what worries me most is his throat and the pool of blood spilling out of it.

If I kill my brother, I will never forgive myself.

Sorrow seeps deep into my bones, and I try whistling, but wheeze from lungs punctured by a bone. He doesn't respond, and his eyes open and close slowly. Too slowly. In bird, we blink quickly, so quickly, nobody even notices we're doing it, and in flight, we blink often to ease the pressure on the eyes and make them less watery.

I whistle-wheeze again, and a tiny whine escapes his open beak. His tongue hangs to the side. Blood flows freely out of his neck and onto the rock, reaching my beak. I inhale the scent, and a wail rips out of me. My broken ribs jab my lungs even more. Pain makes me see black. I'm blinking it away, trying to stay awake even though I'll heal faster if I rest.

I need to stop his bleeding. I need to hunt for the Omega and myself. If I don't, I fear my own hunger during our coupling. I fear I will consume her. She is delicious in every way. Flesh and soul, tempting my primal instincts, ones predators often indulge in and can't control.

In bird, we heal faster than in male, but that means I don't have hands. I can't transition now and use my hands to cover my brother's wound and pinch his skin over it, holding it there so the skin seals the wound. I try moving my body toward him.

He's watching me, not even blinking anymore.

I grieve for my brother.

Is he really dead?

No, he can't be.

My right ribs crack as I scoot toward him and place my wing over his throat wound while sliding my other wing under his body to lift his head so he'll have a cushion and not pass into the next world alone. I peep, wishing he could understand me, wishing I could tell him I didn't mean to attack him, I didn't mean to go for his throat and bleed him to death.

"Brother," I call out but in bird. It comes out a whistle.

Diwi swallows, and because my wing is under him, I feel it. He's still alive, but not for long.

"Nen!" Ila calls from above.

I try whistling.

Can she hear me?

She whistles back.

I whistle again, a long sorrowful sound, and it occurs to me that her mother might be walking again as well. A goddess of fertility, of life, of birth and rebirth. And so I pray this strange yet cute and lost prey that is Ila, my Omega, will reach for her mother and ask her to spare my brother and give him another chance at life.

We've died in great numbers over the past decade of wars. Surely Ila won't want me or my brother to die. If only he'd known the human I captured wasn't food but a breeder and a goddess in her own right, he never would've tried to attack.

My brother and I share everything, even our food. We always have. The pair of us are not territorial toward each other, and he probably thought I'd caught a nice snack he and I could share. If we die, Ila will surely starve up there.

The Om males doing the daily rounds have already finished sweeping this part. They won't return until dawn, when it will be too late to save either of us. They might consume her.

"Mother." Ila's voice drifts down to me. "Call on Eme." Eme? Oh no, don't call on Eme! All my feathers stand on end. Nobody prays to Eme, for Eme is fond of bleeding predators.

"My dear cousin, Eme," Ila says, and I lift my head and try screeching at her to stop. Eme is the last goddess I want her to call right now. With my keen eye, I spot the Om-las coming out of their huts, noses lifted and moving, ears erect and twitching. Winds blow her scent and voice to them, and they'll find out I've yet to consume the prey I caught a while back. They might try to take her from me. I screech again to keep Ila quiet.

But no, Ila prays quietly, even though the winds carry her voice across the lands, reaching another goddess that I sure hope isn't Eme. "Take their blood sacrifice, but let them live," Ila says. "If you bleed them, that which you desire the most will never happen. I know what you desire the most, and I will take it from you. Spare them, Eme, or I will take revenge."

I swallow. Goddesses are vicious even when they're family. Can't they all be nice and ask for favors instead of threatening each other? Bera is Eme's aunt. Bera delivered Eme, the Bloodletter, out of Herea's womb with her own two hands, and has blessed Eme with female offspring. Ila is Eme's cousin.

It occurs to me, Ila must really like me if she's threatening Eme. It's really neither here nor there at the moment, but it's nice to know.

Down in the village, the Om-las are listening. Their Sha-male is climbing the hill to stand on two feet, in male, with his staff pointed to the sky. The winds sweep the mountain-side, clear the skies, and echo Ila's voice. I have a bad feeling. I think Ila's trying to reach both Bera and Eme across the lands, which means Eme is walking again, which means goddesses are coming back to take predators as lovers. To use us, twist us, play with us, and once they grow bored, they will abandon us.

Not Ila, though. I knotted and bonded her to me. She won't be able to resist me or escape me. My scent will tie her to me and to our lands until the end of our time.

Ila chants in an ancient language.

The Sha-male is repeating her words, shouting them from the hill at the top of his lungs. I'm sure he's excited. The Sha-males worship goddesses and preserve our faith.

The winds gather into a storm, lifting my feathers, and the blood from my brother's neck wound starts retreating back into my brother's body. It is the most unsettling thing I've ever witnessed. Eme has granted him a boon.

And so I also pray. I pray until my throat is parched and my tongue is numb, and even though I'm whining and whistling, I'm speaking, moving my tongue and throat muscles in the way I would in male. I pray until a trance takes me under. Tired, I sleep, praying my brother will live, for he cannot die at the end of my beak.

* * *

I awake with a jolt, and the first thing I see is my brother hovering over me. Joy courses through me like a living thing, and I spring up, fluff out my wings.

Diwi strikes my beak. Once, twice, three times, and screeches at me as he rises to his full height. He spreads his wings, feathers all standing on end.

Well, the good ones. There's a patch of missing feathers under his neck where I ripped into him. The wound healed, but his entire belly is covered in crusted blood.

His fitness is not at optimum, I'd say.

He pokes my beak again, and I bow my head, telling him I'm sorry for attacking him. He could kill me now. Strike my skull and pierce it with the sharp edge of his beak. But unlike me, he won't try to kill his brother on purpose.

Oh. What's that? There's splattered paint on his talons, and I catch sight of a paintbrush. Whatever for?

Unfortunately, my brother being alive poses a different problem. My brother is an Om male, and he will want to meet Ila. Everyone in the village below will want to meet Ila too.

Turning, I see the Om-las already climbing the mountain. The pilgrimage has started. I'm not ready for anyone to see her. Maybe I'll never be ready. She's all mine, and I'm feeling terribly territorial.

Eme ought to bleed me some more. The only reason she spared me is because Eme loves her aunt and Ila is Bera's daughter. Or maybe Ila threatening Eme is how things get done in goddessland.

The Om-las Sha-male knows Ila has returned. He will send word of her return to every female Omega in our territory. They will come, pay homage to Ila, and linger around her, for when she goes into heat, the other Omegas might also start theirs. Omegas not going into heat has been the plague of our wars, of Bera not giving us any young.

I land on my platform, and shortly after, my brother follows at my tail. Pausing before I enter, I glance back at him, annoyed he's following me inside my lair, and unless I attack him again, no amount of dissuasion is gonna put him off.

He saw the prey I've captured, heard the prayer, and he's coming to investigate. While I am the Omi of my people, I can order them to do anything I want and they will do it. Because I am the Omi of my people, I'm also responsible for their well-being. My brother investigating Ila is something I have to allow.

Nevertheless, I fight the urge to kill him and pick off the pilgrims on their way up.

Diwi shrieks.

I cannot kill my brother. I can't kill my own people, land predators or otherwise. I must become a male so I'm not so territorial and aggressive.

I transition to male and return to the nest, where I find Ila pacing. She stops and smiles. "It worked!" she says and rushes up the steps. I barely have time to catch her as she flings her body at me and wraps her fragile arms around me, kissing my cheek and mouth and nose. A stranger to outpourings of female affection, I stand there, a statue.

Ila looks up, a question in her gaze. I don't believe she even saw Diwi. This makes me think she can only see her Omi and no other male, and I smirk, placing her on the ground. Near the nest, I find my flimsy cloth and tie it over my hips. I'm gonna need to hit Ralna's markets and actually get clothes.

I haven't thought about clothes or shaving or jewelry or anything a male or a female would want for so many turns, I'm utterly unprepared for my goddess or her pilgrims. She came to me, claimed her home, and claimed her Omi male. I returned the claim and knotted her, bonding her to me. My entire life is changing before my eyes, and I need to hurry up and acclimate.

Back at the platform inside the home, I motion my brother forward and into the nesting space from the hallway. "Female, this is my brother, Diwi. Diwi meet Ila. She has returned and rides the winds again."

My brother stares at me, and I note he's carrying a sack.

Ila extends her hand.

Now we both stare at her hand, arm bent at an angle.

"We shake hands when we meet new people," she says. "Or when we see them again."

Diwi turns his head in profile and side-eyes her like a bird might, and Ila drops her hand to her hip.

"Let's talk in the sitting room," I say and lead the way.

"There's a sitting room?" Ila asks.

The sitting room is a part of a large housing unit complex with several rooms, none of which I use for sitting. Mainly, it's where my bird dumps things I find interesting, like the last crashed alien ship "sitting" in the corner collecting dust.

Bones, weapons, and the like litter the floor. But the light bugs are here. They only come into rooms where a person is moving, so someone has been here before. Ah, this is where Ila got the extra pelts for the nest.

I walk to the pile in the left corner and start rummaging through it until I get to the bottom, pretty sure that's where the logs and some furnishings are, but hit the ground instead, finding nothing of use to sit on.

I move to the next corner.

"Nen?" Ila says.

"In a moment." Where is my fucking shit? I kick the Ka-made bowl, and it bounces off the wall and hits me in the head. I catch it in my hands and wanna bite the gold for being so strong and well crafted. The Ka are known for their crafts. Too bad the Ra nearly exterminated them, and the Ka forgot their arts in favor of military and strategic survival training.

I find two logs. Ila sits on one, and I stand behind her, crossing my arms over my chest, clearly offering my brother a sitting place across from her on the other side of the room.

My brother remains in the shadows. He's on two feet and lingering by the entrance, and when the bugs start to come to life near him, he retreats, unwilling to show himself. "There're some throws around here if you want to cover your middle," I say. I doubt he would. The female can assess his fitness faster if she sees it. I'm not intimidated by my brother's fitness. One, my dick is the biggest dick in the lands, and two, Ila is mine.

I'm unafraid she'll find him more fit, though I'm feeling territorial at the same time. The issue I have now, besides not finding logs or sitting pelts for myself, is that my brother is rather handsome, with an easy smile.

The three scars running down my jaw make me a bit... uglier. "Why are you here?" I snap at him, then sigh in annoyance with myself. My brother is always welcome in my home. What's gotten into me? I glance at the goddess, who's looking between us.

My brother is keeping to the shadows where bugs aren't as active yet.

"What are you doing?" I ask him.

"Nothing."

"I see that, Diwi. Come and sit."

When he doesn't, I say, "I'm sorry for attacking you."

"I see why you did."

"It's not an excuse," I say.

My brother walks forward, passing me the sack he'd brought in. I go to get it, but he pulls his hand back.

"It's not for you," he says.

I frown and step away to see what he'll do.

Diwi drops to one knee and places the sack at Ila's feet.

She digs inside, pulling out brushes, paints, an entire scripting kit.

"You were looking for paints. These are fresh," he says.

"Diwi," I ask, my voice a warning, "have you met Ila before?"

He locks eyes with her, and she smiles, and I am going to kill him. I walk around her with the intention of grabbing him and pounding his face with my fist when Ila places a gentle hand over my forearm. "He brings gifts."

"Another male cannot provide for you," I snap.

She lifts her chin. "And why not?"

"Because I said so."

Ila's eyes narrow. "And what of the pilgrims? Will you strike them all?"

"Yes."

She chuckles. "They're bringing gifts too. You said Ila is a big deal, and where I come from, stories of pagan goddesses say the goddesses take sacrifices. It is the same on Nomra Prime. I don't need a sacrifice. I prefer gifts. Jewelry, clothing, paints, materialistic stuff. Handmade, preferably. Did you make the bowl, Diwi?"

"No," I answer as Diwi rises to stand near Ila as if she's a magnet, drawing him into what could still be his death at my hands. "This kind of work comes from the Ka tribe." I swipe the obsidian bowl from the floor and point at the gold that keeps the broken pieces of this antique object together. "The Ka sculpt with gold and serrion."

"It's very pretty," Ila says. "Thank you for bringing me the paints."

Why can't I kill him? Or all the males collectively?

Diwi sits and spreads his legs as if we're alone and the cock hanging between his thighs is of no importance.

Ila looks away. As she should.

I shrug off her extra pelt and throw it at him. "Dress."

He smirks. "Yes, Omi."

Oh, fuck him. He hasn't called me an Omi since I became one. I am so irate right now, I can't have a normal conversation.

"Won't you sit down?" he suggests.

"No."

He chuckles. "You do understand I can't steal Ila from the Omi, and especially now that she's been mated."

"Yes," I snap.

"Relax."

"I *am* relaxed." I stand behind her, crossing my arms over my chest. "See? Relaxing, standing back here like a little bug on the wall."

He shakes his head. "I found the bowl on Ka territory just over Gension Heights."

"And you stole it?" I ask.

"Mmhm."

"Did anyone see you?"

"An alien like this one saw me."

"What?" Ila says. "A woman saw you?"

He nods.

"Well, go on," she says. "What happened?"

"She waved." My brother makes a gesture identical to the one Ila used when I asked to test her eyesight, which is terrifyingly terrible, and I will spend the rest of my life in fear someone will snatch her before she can summon wind to defend herself.

"She just waved at you?" Ila asked.

Diwi nods.

"That's unusual," Ila says. "Normally, we'd run at the sight of you."

"That's because this one is mad," he says.

I frown, but he continues, and pieces begin to fall into place.

"At the same time, Ila crashed, another woman crashed, but in Ka territory," Diwi says. "They held games, and the Ra alpha won."

"That's not good." We can't afford another war, and Ark winning in Hart's territory is surely a cause for war.

"That's the thing, brother. Hart marked the womankind. She is Amti, goddess of madness and lust."

"Of madness and lust," Ila repeats and starts chanting, "Amti, Amti, Amti."

My brother stands and scratches his nose, cheek, back of his neck. I step away. Discomfort develops as an itch on my belly too. If I were bird, my feathers would bristle.

Ila turns to me, eyes white like mine, and stunned, I stare.

"We have returned," she says. "I can feel the others."

"Where?" Diwi asks.

"Here."

"Here where?" I ask.

"In the mountain."

I crouch before Ila. "There are females in the mountain?"

"And elsewhere."

"Goddesses?"

"Not all."

"But they're all prey we can breed like you?"

"Women. We are women."

"I'll alert the scouts. Every male will take to the skies. We will find them, bring them here," Diwi says.

"No," Ila snaps. "They shouldn't be brought here."

"Why not?" I ask.

"Because no other goddess shall make a home on my mountain."

And here I thought *I* was too territorial.

"The Om females are flying in. One is almost here." Ila

gets up and walks out of the sitting room. My brother and I linger. We exchange a look. We've never dealt with divinity before, and it's both fear inducing and hopeful.

"We should gather wood for the fire. The Sha-male will need it," Diwi says. He claps my shoulder. "Bathe before you receive the tribemates. You smell like pussy."

"Omega pussy," I correct.

"Shall we meet her?" Ila's head pokes around the corner, and I swear to Ila (need to find another goddess to swear on now), I almost startle.

My brother and I follow Ila outside, and she points a finger up and to her right. "Over there."

"There's nothing there," I say, terrified of her poor eyesight. Her eyes are white like mine now, so why can't she see as well as I can?

Moments later, something blue flashes in the sky. "There. I see a bird. Do you?" I ask her.

"No, but I know she's there."

"How do you know?"

"The wind is in her favor."

My brother birds-up and shakes out his tail, anticipating the female landing. When she lands in a flurry of midnight-blue underfeathers, he whistles. She whistles back, and I've never felt more blessed and grateful to the goddesses than I do now. My tribe will have young.

EPILOGUE

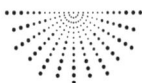

NEN

I spy with my eye something round and welcome. It's Ila's belly. Across the room, I'm trying to enjoy my view when three males bring gifts and sit down with my goddess. Intruders. I hate them, but these are my tribemates seeking blessings, and I'm trying (very hard) to suppress my feelings. Namely, I feel like killing them all.

They're talking about the history of the gifts they hand made. All of a fucking sudden, every male in the Om tribe, land or sky predator, is skilled with his hands. Gifted artists, Ila praises them and pats her big belly.

The belly is nice. I smile. She thinks she'll deliver babies. The young shall be born inside eggs, which will provide them with nutrients until they hatch as babies and can nurse from her breasts, which have doubled in size since her pregnancy began. *Blessed Bera.*

A male scoots closer to my goddess.

Sitting in the corner of the common room, I'm sharpening my third dagger, eyeing the male with Ila, waiting, just waiting for him to make a move. He won't, but I'm paranoid and dislike all the males who are lingering in my house.

They've all brought gifts, some more than one. Instead of dumping them all in the corners, Ila arranges the gifts on shelves and displays them for all to see. She says a display of fine crafts in her home makes everyone happy, makes tribemates feel like she appreciates the gifts.

I still want to kill them. All eighty-seven Alpha males inside my home, who are, in packs, breeding Omega females. All the rooms are taken, because when females visit Ila, they have no time to fly to their nests before the heat hits. They go into heat instantly, and so the males have started taking up rooms in my large dwelling. The females build nests, then fuss over the arrangement, and once the female's nest is ready, the breeding can start.

My previously deserted house is an Om breeding ground.

Solitude is no longer in the future for me, mainly because I'll soon have young and also because Ila is a highly social creature. She spends lots of time talking with strangers.

I hate strangers, and some of these males are strangers and they're all intruding, and if that one motherfucker moves any closer to her or touches her hair, I'm gonna stab him in the eye.

Life is changing for me, and I'm trying to adjust. I am trying. Really. I pull back my hand and throw the dagger.

It flies past the male's head and hits the wall, bouncing back and clinking to the ground.

All three of the males sitting with Ila scamper out the door. Calmly, I walk toward my dagger, eyeing another pack on the right as I swipe my blade off the ground and start cleaning my claws with it. They get a clue and leave as well.

Ila smiles, a glint in her eye. "Something ruffling your feathers, Alpha?"

"People. Too many of them." I extend a hand to help her up. She groans as she rises, and I pat her belly. "Almost. The young will come soon."

MILANA JACKS

She shakes her head. "Human babies cook for nine months."

When one of my tribemates found a woman like Ila running around the fields, I flew to Ka territory for a translator, and I saw the Ka cooking their prey. At the time, I didn't understand. I understand now since Ila explained humans cook their food before eating it. Do they eat their young? This is terrible news.

"Nen, are you okay?"

"No. Not at all. Cooking young is not acceptable." Nine cycles of cooking! *Hello, Bera, mother of all, are you listening?*

Ila laughs. "Not in a literal sense. It takes nine months for the baby to develop and be ready for the world."

Another case of terrible human jargon. "You aren't having human babies."

She bites her bottom lip, then whispers, "What if there's something wrong with them?"

Ah. I envelop her in a hug. "They will be healthy and strong. Don't worry."

Ila kisses my chest, and my dick hardens. I kiss the top of her head, then trail my lips down her cheek to her lips, coaxing them to open.

"I need fresh air," she says, then pulls away and marches out of the room.

What the fuck?

Of course, I'm right behind her. There're males in the house, and she's not allowed to go anywhere alone. I'm her fucking shadow. She thinks I'm not there, but I'm everywhere she is at all times, vigilantly protecting her from foes, imaginary or otherwise.

On the platform, Ila's still walking.

"What are you doing?" I pick up my pace, then run as I see her spread her arms and jump off the cliff. My body explodes into my bird, and I shoot down after her, then hit a gust of wind. It throws me back up, and I bat my wings, fighting it with all my might, frantically turning my neck every which way, looking for her.

"Ila!" I screech.

"Over here." A whisper comes from inside the gusts of wind battering my body.

I turn. Ila stands back on the platform, waving.

I land on two feet beside her and grit my teeth. I open my mouth to argue with her, but she rises on her toes and kisses me. She slides her tongue into my mouth and twirls it the way I like and the way she knows gets me excited. But I have to stand firm. Pulling back, I ask, "Why did you jump?"

My Omega smiles. "A human can't fly, Nen. I've always been afraid of heights. Hell, most of us are. I just wanted to... know, for certain, that I can actually summon wind, and when my babies grow, I want to know I can fly with them. Anywhere. Across this entire land."

"You could've warned me."

"I wanted to do it on my own."

"Next time, you will tell me," I order. Claws digging into her ass cheeks, I pick her up and walk back inside to the nest, where I try (even though I know I can't) to add another young inside her.

Bera blessed the Om again, and I hope one day, I can be the male to bring her gifts. I think a grandbaby will do.

***

OMG, how I loved Nen, let me count the ways! Funny, knotty, naughty, jealous, possessive, territorial... all the things that make up a great Alpha male in a Milana story. I hope you loved him too. Who's next? Read the introduction to the Ra tribe on the next page.

CONSUMED TEASER

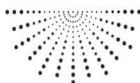

TASH

*M*y balls itch. Half awake, I turn onto my back and scratch them, move them around to get them unstuck from each other, weigh them in my hand a bit, thinking about jerking off, then deciding not to.

I wonder why my balls itch in the morning. Do all males get itchy down there in the morning? Why morning and not evening? Have I been itching in the evening too?

Human footsteps pad over the wooden floors and toward the back of the house, disrupting my high-level intellectualizing on my itchy balls. Since I'm testing my sense of smell for recognizing these human females that are roaming my house during all hours of the span, I keep my eyes shut.

The female slides open the partition separating my bed from the rest of the house. Colorful metal beads making up the sheer partition click against each other as she enters my chambers. She stops at the bench on my right.

I inhale and sort out my senses. My balls start itching again, and while my hand is down there, I scratch some more, grunting when my dick leaks fluid. I don't jerk off to human scents, not even this one who smells like fresh spring lanever, a gentle lilla-colored flower that grows near my old home in Ralna.

The scent reminds me of the times when peace ruled the lands. My mother would take me by my hand while carrying wee Ark into the fields where we could run in hunter. Ark would eat the lanever and throw up. I would collect the flowers for my mother.

Back when she still loved me.

Back when she wasn't bitter over Dad's death.

Back when my stepbrother hadn't poisoned her mind.

"Use a different flower when you bathe from now on," I say, voice still sleepy and gruff. I know which female this is.

"That's the only flower that's rich in oils and doesn't dry my hair," she says.

I peel open my eyes and turn my head toward where the female with curly dark hair tipped in yellow folds my leather belts on the bench.

"I brought you breakfast," she says.

The females Ark and I kept for the males in my earldom are trying to change the way we do things. We're not the Ka. I'm not gonna change my ways. "I eat out."

"It's game day three, and you haven't hunted in a while. Eat the food I brought."

Amused, I turn on my side, prop a hand under my head, and size up the female who has taken to fixing my house. She asked to be excused from the games. When I refused because every female must be bred, she offered her services. Apparently, the female is what they call an interior designer, and humans pay her to arrange useless things in their homes.

I am a simple male. I need a bed, which I have and…a female in my bed. This one is ripe, mature, maybe about my age, well into forty turns, with wide hips, a narrow waist, and ample breasts. She wears a white cotton robe over her brown skin and jewelry on her ears and arms like our own females do. My sac fills, and my body awakens for the span. Groaning, I fist myself, but don't stroke.

I like big females. Older females. Females with scarred souls and minds that offer conversation based on spans of life experience. This one fits. She's scarred. I can tell. Guarded yet kind. She's everything I find attractive, but I won't invite a human into my bed, not even if it means I'll never have heirs.

While our goddesses haven't taken up residence within all the human females, they have inspirited some. The Ka have marked and impregnated at least four. Rumor has it Ila finally visited the Omi, and the Omi is now completely obsessed with her. He almost killed his brother when the brother tried to gift Ila with paint. Fucking paint.

I love my little brother, and I don't intend to obsess over a goddess and want to kill him. Therefore, Ark and I gave most of the human females we seized from the human cruiser to the Ka. It was Ark's strategic decision, one I agree with, mainly because it makes the Ra less vulnerable to the goddesses running our lives, and also because gifting them to the Ka puts us in Hart's favor.

Hart is a mighty fighter—I'd know; I fought him once and almost died—and he'll come to our aid when Ark returns to Ralna and causes mayhem against an enemy far more powerful than my brother. Not in size or fitness, because Ark is the most agile of predators, an Alpha of the Ra, but an enemy whose power has grown in Ark's absence.

"Why are you bringing me food and folding my iertos?"

She shrugs. "You promised me freedom from the games."

"Why don't you want to mate?" I prop myself up on the bed. "Is our collective fitness offensive to you?" Does she think the Ka pussies are better-looking than us? Because they're not. Bar that one blondie, my males are far more handsome than the Ka, Hart in particular. Ugly bastard to be sure.

"I don't need a reason for not wanting to mate anyone."

"You don't need to tell me the reason, but you sure as fuck have one." I wait for a retort, but she doesn't respond. "You're not my servant," I remind her. "I have other females for that."

She snorts. "The pair of Ra females departed about ten days ago. There's nobody left besides Angela, who's busy with the games, Lena, and me. And your males are messier than you are."

"I am not messy."

She giggles.

My brain is foggy in the morning, and I just caught what she said earlier. "What do you mean the Ra females departed?" And who's been caring for my house since? Wow, I hadn't noticed.

"Left. Abandoned posts. Said there's a bad smell coming from you."

I sniff my armpit. "I should probably bathe."

"Lena is bathing in the private baths now. Please don't disturb her."

Lena is this one's human pet. She's hovered over the younger girl since we boarded them on our warbird. She even shares food with Lena and puts her to bed. I asked if the girl is her child, and Imani laughed, said she doesn't have children and the girl isn't a child anymore. Then Imani got sad and cried because the girl celebrated her birthday on the ship with rations and a prayer instead of having the big party most eighteen-year-olds like to hold.

We left plenty of food.

The warbird can sustain life for over a turn.

I don't know why the humans couldn't throw a party. It makes me wonder about them. For a predator, there's nothing worse than captivity. We go feral, mad inside the holes in the ground or cages.

At the thought of pacing a small dark space, a growl builds in my throat, and the female freezes, her back to me.

I smell her fear and promptly plug my nose. My belly growls. "You're right, female," I say in a soft albeit nasal voice because I don't dare breathe in her scent, which is that of both prey and female, lanever in the fields and flesh under my gums.

"Out with you," I order. "I'm hungry."

She scurries outside, and I unplug my nose, then breathe in the mix of delicate prey and the blood of ravaged predators in the fields. I love both, and stick my tongue out as if trying to taste the air. Instead of eating whatever she bought for me, I tend to the raging hormones accumulated in my balls. I stroke my length only twice and cum all over the sheets. Sweet Bera, mother of all, these human females can't leave my home soon enough. I gotta get rid of them as fast as possible. Good thing I only have two left. This one and her pet, neither of whom are presenting like goddesses. *Get your copy today!*

MILANA'S BACKLIST

Tribes:

Marked #1, Stolen #2, Lured #3, Captured #4, Consumed #5

Read the complete Beast Mates Series:

#0 Virgin - FREEBIE, #1 Blind, #2 Wild,

#2.5 Goddess, FREE via my Mailing List,

#3 Sent, #3.5 Their, #4 Caught, #4.5 His, #5 Free.

Read the Complete Horde Series:

#1 Alpha Breeds, #2 Alpha Bonds, #3 Alpha Knots, #4 Alpha Collects

The Complete Hordesmen Series:

Hunger #1, Terror #2, Sidone #3, Fever #4, Dreikx #5, The Blind Hordesman #6

Read the complete Dragon Brotherhood:

Rise #1, Burn #2, Storm #3, Fight, #4

Short stories in IADB World: Jake 1.5, Eddy #2.5

Read the complete Age of Angels series:

Court of Command, #1 • Court of Sunder, #2 • Court of Virtue, #3

ABOUT THE AUTHOR

Milana Jacks grew up with tales of water fairies that seduced men, vampires that seduced women, and Babaroga who'd come to take her away if she didn't eat her bean soup. She writes sci-fi fantasy romance with dominant monsters from her home on Earth she shares with Mate and their three little beasts.

• Sometimes she releases stories for the readers on her mailing list as they await for books in the series. If you want in, join other readers at http://www. milanajacks.com/newsletter/ •

Meet me at
www.milanajacks.com

Printed in Great Britain
by Amazon